Cowboys, Castles and Cradles

Loralee Lillibridge

By Loralee Lillibridge

© 2017 Loralee Lillibridge
Swartz Creek, MI 48473

Tell-Tale Publishing Group, LLC
5471 Peri Street
Swartz Creek, MI 48737   TT Imprint

Remembering cowboys and rodeos, boots and Texas two-stepping, bluebonnets and Longhorns.

This book is for Kay Tilton, my special Texas friend through the years. Many thanks for your help with this story.

Chapter One

Texas Hill Country - Summer

If Whitman C. Lovett the Third hadn't missed his turn on the winding Texas Hill Country road during the sudden thunderstorm, he might never have seen the commotion taking place in the tree-dotted pasture.

The treacherous stretch of blacktop called Devil's Backbone couldn't have been more aptly named. When multiple hair-pin curves began following every belly-dropping dip in the road after he turned off I-35, he'd shot right past the road sign he'd been looking for instead of paying attention to where he was going. His obsession with leaving the family business for so long was eating away at him. Now he was back-tracking, cussing and wondering where his good sense had gone.

Angry at his lack of foresight for not checking the weather advisory before he left San Antonio, Whit's disposition simmered just below the boiling point. All he wanted right now was to forget the whole ugly mess with his father and brother and head for the nearest hotel. Maybe crash for a couple of hours and give his weary brain cells a rest. As tired as he was, he'd even settle for one of those chain-owned inns that dotted the sides of I-35, as long as the sheets were clean and there was plenty of hot water for a shower.

He'd left the Texas City headquarters of Lovett Geological Survey, Inc. at four o'clock this morning in order to meet his father and brother for an early business breakfast at the

Company's branch office in San Antonio. The entire meeting had been one big argument over the terms of the impending land lease he was supposed to acquire for the next LGS geological survey.

Prior to the meeting, his brother, Brody, had laid out the detailed results of his independent study of the area to their father. Leasing three thousand acres of the Castle ranch that adjoined the three thousand acres leased earlier from another ranch would complete the acquisition needed for a successful geological play.

Whit's negotiating skill was all that was needed now to make the deal happen and end his obligation to the family company permanently.

Tired, hungry and still smarting from his father's latest bargaining scheme, the only thing he wanted right now was to

locate the owner of Castle Ranch as soon as possible, seal the deal and get on with the rest of his life. The life he'd been planning for the last three years.

Hunched over the steering wheel, he squinted through the *whap-whap* of the wipers hoping to spot some sign of assurance that he was on the right road. The sheet of slanting rain on the pickup's windshield cut visibility to less than the length of his headlight beam. He damn sure didn't want to go over the steep embankment, so he eased back on the accelerator and tried not to overreact.

He wasn't afraid to take a risk now and then, but he wasn't stupid. Risking his neck and risking his money were two different matters. He happened to like his neck right where it was. His money . . . well, he had more than enough to cover what he had in mind for the future and then some. All he had to do was stick around long enough to make his plan happen.

A bright red 2:15 glowed on the digital dashboard clock, but the dark clouds and heavy rain had already turned the early afternoon into a gloomy gray. Whit swore and clenched his jaw so tight his back teeth ached. This trip just kept getting worse and worse. Next time he'd remember to check the weather report before he took off. Correction—there'd be no next time. No more arguments with his father and younger brother. As soon as he wrapped up this Castle ranch deal, he was out of here. Damn straight!

Lightning flashed again, revealing the road sign he'd been watching for. He swung the half-ton Silverado to the left, relieved to finally be headed in the right direction, albeit much later than he'd originally planned. Five miles later, the wisdom of his decision was definitely in question. *Reminder to self, replace broken GPS when I get back to Texas City.* He should've followed his first instinct and stayed in San Antonio.

As he passed a marker confirming he was still on the right road, a movement in the field caught his eye.

What the . . . ?

Rain blurred the windshield, making it difficult to see clearly. Still squinting, he slowed the truck. Sure enough, someone was out there in the pouring rain. No one in their right mind would stand under a tree like a human lightning rod in this kind of storm, for cryin' out loud.

Another spear of lightning sizzled beside a huge live oak, flooding the field with a halogen-like blue glow. Whit sucked in his breath. Was he seeing things? He blinked twice just to be sure he wasn't hallucinating. He wasn't.

A woman, obviously lacking her share of safety smarts, struggled with a bellowing cow determined not to go anywhere.

"Of all the . . . " Whit crimped the steering wheel, hit the brakes and skidded to a stop on the side of the rain-slicked road, all in a single motion.

"Crazy lady," he muttered, shooting out of the truck right before the door slammed behind him. "Good way to get killed."

A high-pitched scream, not unlike that of an injured animal, split the air and sent chills crawling along Whit's spine. Swearing as he ran, he vaulted the wooden rail fence, with a heartfelt *thanks* to the Almighty for the absence of any emasculating barbed wire strung along the top. His boots hit the ground on the other side hard enough to jar his insides, but he didn't slow down. After seconds that seemed to last for hours, he reached the woman's side, ready to rescue her from whatever imminent danger prompted her call for help.

"What's wrong? Are you hurt?" If his breath hadn't been painfully jammed in his chest around his pounding heart, he might have asked if she was waiting for Noah's Ark to float by, but he didn't. For the life of him, he didn't see any reason for her to be screaming at a cow when she should've been heading for the safety of her home . . . wherever that might be. The woman looked like she'd been swimming in a water tank, but at least he didn't see any visible signs of injuries.

"Everything is wrong!" She yelled at him like all this was his fault. "In case you haven't noticed, I'm trying to get this heifer out of the pasture. Does it look like I'm having a picnic?"

Two almond–shaped green eyes glittered from under the brim of a soggy canvas hat that had apparently been snitched from a scarecrow. Corkscrew strands of dark auburn hair poked out from beneath it in all directions. The woman pushed a muddy hand at the curls plastered to her forehead and skewered Whit with an icy look that could've kept a case or two of longnecks cold for a week. Well, damn.

Whit took in the woman's soggy appearance with one sweeping glance. No wonder she was mad. Good old Texas mud splattered her from head to toe. Her strange-looking plaid shirt was about two sizes too big and her jeans—what he could see of them underneath the hem of that baggy shirt—were mud-covered, too. She didn't look much better than the half-drowned critter on the ground, its huge, liquid-brown eyes staring at them accusingly.

He couldn't tell what was behind the smudges on her face, but she looked a bit younger than he'd first thought. Not that it mattered. He opened his mouth to comment on her predicament when another clap of thunder startled the animal into a bellowing tug-of-war with her captor. The rope slipped from the woman's hands.

"Help!"

Whit lunged, threw his arms around the critter's neck and dug his heels in the mud. Slipping and sliding, he finally brought the heifer to a halt, but not before he was as mud-covered as the woman.

His Stetson shifted cockeyed over one eye. He jerked it off, rubbed unsuccessfully at the chunks of mud splattered on it, then shoved it back in place. Great. Now his new, custom-made hat would have to be completely cleaned and re-blocked. A swift inspection of his jeans and boots confirmed his fear. He looked like he'd been herding cattle through the Rio Grande.

"You're absolutely right, ma'am," he said in all sincerity, when his breathing finally returned to normal and his voice didn't sound like he'd been huffing helium balloons. "This is definitely not a picnic."

The woman eyed him suspiciously. "Well, what are you doing out here?"

Whit couldn't stop his grin, in spite of the rain in his face. "That was going to be *my* next question to you, ma'am."

My, oh my, she was a sight to behold, prickly as the cactus scattered over the field and pretty as its blossoms. Even mud-covered from head to toe, her pixie-like beauty was hard to ignore. He wasn't quite sure what was up with the baggy clothes, though. His experience with women's fashions consisted of paying the exorbitant bills for his ex's designer outfits, not to mention her closet full of shoes.

"Clementine needs to be in the barn before she has her calf."

"Calf? As in giving birth to one?" Whit looked from the woman to the animal and back again. Sure enough, the cow's stomach was suspiciously round. Aw, man, what else? He'd witnessed a similar event once at his grandparents' small ranch outside of Kerrville, but he'd been a youngster then, just a wide-eyed observer of the actual birth. What he remembered of the process wasn't pretty.

"Of course, birth. Where do you think calves come from? The cow fairy?" She arched an eyebrow at him and fisted her hands on her hips. "Are you sure you're a cowboy?"

He hadn't claimed any such thing, so why would she think that? An explanation was on the tip of Whit's tongue, but he choked on it when his gaze landed on another four-legged critter staring at them from the far side of the field.

Holy . . . ! Disaster with a capital D. No, make that B, as in bull.

Wide as a battleship and boasting horns like deadly bayonets, the bull lowered its head and pawed the ground, leaving no doubt in Whit's mind what would happen the minute he made a wrong move.

The woman kept chattering, unaware.

" . . . and the blessed event will take place right out here in the pouring rain unless I can get her back to the barn before dark. I can't let that happen."

Whit only heard part of what the flame-haired sprite was telling him and none of it registered in his busy brain. The bull's threatening bellow had his full attention and he grabbed for the woman's hand.

"Ma'am, we've got to get out of here, pronto."

She jerked her hand from his. "That's exactly what I've been trying to do," she said, her cheeks flushed from what Whit guessed was exertion. "And she's a heifer until she has the calf."

Wrestling four-legged bovines wasn't exactly child's play, as he'd just learned, but now wasn't the time for more lessons in cow-speak.

Two of her shirt buttons came undone, giving Whit a more personal look at the pint-sized redhead as she fumbled to fix them. He was unprepared for the next shock, one that damn near stopped his already racing heart. Unless she was hiding a watermelon underneath that shirt, this damsel-in-distress was one very pregnant lady. And that put a whole new spin on the situation.

Icy fear clutched Whit's gut as his survival mode kicked into high speed. What kind of mess had he gotten himself into? A two-ton bull eyed them suspiciously from across the pasture and this expectant mom was obviously in no condition to run for safety. Did he look like a super hero?

Without asking permission, he yanked his hat down around his ears, scooped the woman up in his arms and ran like the devil was nipping at his heels, which was way too close to the truth to give him much hope of survival.

"Put me down! Are you crazy?" She pounded her fists against his shoulder. "I can't leave Clementine out there."

"Lady, that heifer's not the one in danger right now. We are." Whit didn't dare slow down to see if the bull was gaining on them, even though his chest burned with every breath he took. *Don't stop now, Lovett. Just run!* With the woman in his arms and the four-legged brute with horns breathing down his neck, Whit took off like his pants were on fire.

Holding on to the woman was trickier than hanging on to a bunch of wet cats.

"Hey, stop wiggling or you'll slide right out of my arms." Whit didn't even want to think about that scenario, so he hugged her tighter against his chest and ran faster than he thought possible.

"Let go, I said!" She kept right on squirming and pummeling his shoulder. He kept right on making tracks across the pasture.

He tore across the field. "Please be still and don't talk, okay? Try not to .

Aghhh!" and his boots hit a patch of slick, wet grass. Slipping and staggering, he fought to stay upright without dropping his armload of angry femininity and prayed he was still running in the direction of the fence. What else could he do with her well-endowed bosom shoved in his face?

Just as he thought he had matters under control, the nutty woman wrapped her arms around his neck in a death grip and he had to invent a whole new dance step just to keep his feet on the ground.

"Put me down before both of us land on our rears! Are you crazy?"

"Not crazy enough to argue with that bull." Dammit, she'd yelled right in his ear. He shook his head to stop the ringing.

Whit had his own opinion as to which one of them was certifiable, but right now he needed to concentrate on staying upright until they reached the fence. He'd never be able to climb over with her in his arms. He was in good shape, but hey, she was no light-weight.

Reaching the fence, he did some fast thinking. "Can you make it over on your own?"

She flashed him a look that clearly told him what she thought of that question.

He dodged the daggers in her glance, but couldn't escape the next problem——where to put his hands in order to lift her up to reach the top rail. *Aw, what the hell.* With a stifled groan, he gave her nicely-rounded fanny a boost with both hands.

"There you go." For a nano-second he regretted having to remove his hands. Then she yelled at him again and he let go like he'd grabbed hold of the lit end of a match.

"Hey, watch where you put your hands, cowboy. I'm pregnant, not helpless." She reached for the top rail, eased one denim-clad leg over, then the other. After only a brief hesitation, she dropped the short distance to the ground with a soft grunt.

Whit was right behind her mere seconds before the bull thundered up and rammed head on into the fence. Bellowing one last warning to the uninvited intruders in his pastoral playground, the animal tossed its head, snorted his disapproval, and trotted off to find a more sheltered spot in the downpour.

Whit bent over and struggled to catch his breath.

"Hot . . . damn! That . . . was close," he said, gasping for breath.

Raindrops plopped from the brim of his mud-splattered Stetson. He wished he'd worn the old one he kept stashed in the back seat of his truck. A cowboy's hat was serious stuff.

Oh, well, if a hat was all he lost to this surreal experience, he'd consider himself lucky. He glanced at the cause of the craziness, only to find her lazer-like gaze leveled right at him. Cripes, now what?

Breathing hard, she took a wobbly step toward him, one hand supporting her stomach, the other pressed against her back. Whit reached out to steady her, but she pushed his hand away.

"Who do you think you are, cowboy, dragging me around like that? Couldn't you see the gate? I wasn't in any danger until you came charging into the pasture like a madman and got Hercules all riled up." She pointed to the snorting bull on the other side of the fence. "I have to get Clementine into the barn before she has her calf, which is going to happen any minute now from the way she's been carrying on. Now move out of my way. I have to go back and get her. You've wasted enough of my time." She shot him another withering look.

Whit thought about reminding her how he'd just risked life and limb to get her out of harm's way, but she got right in his face and poked him in the chest before he could get the words out.

"Exactly who are you, anyway?" She poked him again.

"Ouch." He backed away from her reach before she could jab him again. "Whit, ma'am. Whit, uh, Carter."

Never keen on using the Lovett name around strangers, Whit learned long ago to take his time revealing his true identity until he knew who he was dealing with. Not that this bedraggled woman presented any threat, but he erred to the side of caution, anyway. Remembering his manners, he touched the brim of his rain-soaked hat with his forefinger. "Sorry there wasn't time for proper introductions back there. Are you okay?" He wiped raindrops off his face.

Suddenly, he was staring. He couldn't help it. Her wet shirt was scrunched up, leaving her belly partially exposed. He tried looking away, but that didn't work. Oh, yeah, she was definitely pregnant. He'd heard her say so earlier, but the reality hadn't registered until now.

He managed to choke out another "Ma'am?" before his mouth went dry.

"I'm as okay as I can be after being hauled around like a sack of feed." She jerked at her shirt when she saw the direction of his gaze. "And here's a little information, cowboy. The bull's name is Hercules and the heifer is Clementine. I'm Gracie and the barn's about a mile north of here." She swiped at the raindrops running down her face and started for the gate, which was close enough to make Whit feel like an idiot for jumping the fence instead of using it. "And yes, I'm pregnant."

"Yeah, I can see that." He managed to get his thoughts rearranged and looked around for a trailer or a farm truck. "So, where's your truck?"

"In the barn with a dead battery. It wasn't raining when I left the ranch, just windy. I thought I had time to walk Clementine home before it rained."

The image of this soaking wet, pregnant woman leading an equally pregnant heifer down the road in a rain storm reinforced Whit's first impression. Oh, yeah. Certifiable.

"Look, you need to get out of this rain. The heifer will be okay for a little longer." At least, he hoped so. What he knew about expectant bovines wouldn't fill a shot glass, and pregnant women were way out of his comfort zone. "Let me take you home. Then your husband or one of your ranch hands can come back with a cattle hauler. That'll be a lot safer and faster than making her walk back." What kind of husband would let his pregnant wife tackle a job like this, anyway?

The emotions crossing her face puzzled him. Without a word, she stuck her chin out and marched off toward his truck, her muddy sneakers making loud, sucking sounds as she squished across the water-soaked ground.

He started to ask about her lack of ranch help, but decided it was none of his business. As far as he was concerned, he couldn't get her home fast enough. She was somebody else's problem, not his.

She must've have read his thoughts. "There is no husband. No ranch hands, either," she stated matter-of-factly, after he had helped her into the cab of the truck, then climbed in on the other side. "You wouldn't happen to be looking for work, would you?"

Whit slid behind the wheel poker-faced to hide his surprise. "No, ma'am, I'm not, but don't worry. I'll go back and get that heifer for you after I take you home." *Who the hell was running her ranch?*

He fastened his seat belt, checked to make sure she'd locked hers. His gaze settled on the slight droop of her shoulders that just minutes ago had been so rigid and straight. Now, slumped against the seat with her head resting against the window, she didn't appear to have any fight left. Shadows of fatigue stained the delicate area beneath her eyes. She looked like a scarecrow with her floppy hat scrunched down on her head, especially with that red-gold hair sticking out from under it in all directions. Vulnerable, a little like Orphan Annie, too, he thought. Not at all like the argumentative spitfire he'd carried across the pasture.

A worrisome voice of caution resounded in the depths of his conscience, accompanied by the unusual urge to protect. He shook it off, not wanting to examine it further. Not wanting to get involved, period.

"What kind of livestock do you raise?" Knowing it was bad manners to ask the size of a rancher's operation, Whit curbed his curiosity and made a stab at small-talk just to be friendly. If she happened to tell him how many acres she owned, he wouldn't object. His eyes and ears were always open for possible land to lease, a habit he'd be more than happy to lose when he left the family business.

"Live . . . what?"

Was she just giving him a hard time? Joking? Her wide-eyed, honest expression made him wonder.

"Yeah, you know—horses, cattle, goats, zebras, monkeys?" He could play the game, too.

"Oh, that." Her laugh was soft, edged with a flippancy not reflected in her serious face. She studied her dirty hands, rubbed them together and wiped them on her jeans. "No, we only have Hercules and one other cow besides Clementine. No horses. We have plenty of room, though, if there was anyone to take care of them. The ranch is big." She rolled her eyes. "About ten sections, I was told, though I'm not sure how big a section is."

Whit glanced over at his oddly disturbing passenger. She didn't know a section was six hundred and forty acres? Didn't realize she owned over six thousand acres? Had she been living in a rabbit hole all her life?

"And you don't have any ranch hands?" He could only think of one good reason for her predicament—money or the lack of it.

"Just Wes and Hutch, but they're too old to do any strenuous work. Mostly, they just sit around and give advice." Little frown lines puckered her forehead. "They're extremely good at that."

A bite of sarcasm tinged her last words, but Whit let it go. Obviously, she had employee issues. Even a ranch the size of hers would need a decent crew of capable cowboys. Still, it wasn't his problem.

"So, the two men are family." It was more a statement than a question, but Whit hoped it would tell him more about the lady's situation. He was well experienced at drawing out information from reluctant landowners.

"No, not exactly." She shook her head, sending out a fine spray of raindrops across the space between them. "They think they are, but they came with the ranch. They live in the bunkhouse."

Came with the ranch? Deciding he'd be better off waiting until he saw the ranch for himself before tackling any more questions, he pulled the truck onto the road. "You said north, right?" The woman's personal problems weren't his worry, but he wasn't a total jerk. He would go back and get the damned heifer like he promised, if this Wes and Hutch pair couldn't.

"Just follow the road," she said with a resigned sigh.

Whit did, but he had a sneaking suspicion the road led to more trouble than he needed.

Chapter Two

Gracie leaned back against the truck's leather-upholstered seat and closed her eyes. She was so tired, she was near tears. Maybe she was foolish to let a stranger bring her home, but she hated storms. She didn't like leaving the frightened heifer out in the rain, though. What if Clementine had her calf before they could get her in the barn? Then she'd have two animals to bring home. Or would they both die out there? She had no idea what to do next. And how was she going to do anything without help? True, the man sitting next to her seemed nice enough. And he had offered to go back for Clementine, but she wasn't sure if he meant it or was simply making polite conversation.

If she hadn't been so wet and so exhausted, she might have seen the humor in his question about a cattle hauler. She chewed her lip and tried to remember if she'd seen anything that might have looked like one sitting around the barn. Not that she knew what one actually looked like. But she had to show Wes and Hutch she could do whatever was expected of her. If she decided to stay at the ranch, she needed to learn how to deal with these types of emergencies.

She hadn't intended to admit she had no husband, but there was really no reason to dodge the truth, even though she disliked sharing personal information with strangers. The two men she jokingly called her 'bunkhouse boys' were no longer physically qualified as wranglers. Besides, there was nothing to wrangle on the ranch unless you counted the darned chickens.

Cautiously, she snuck a look at the cowboy sitting next to her. Oh, he definitely qualified as an up-to-date version of a real Texas cowboy. Earlier, when he'd high-jumped the fence and rushed to her rescue, she'd been too surprised to take a good look at him. They were both soaked to the skin, but she couldn't help noticing he looked a lot better than she did. The wet hair she'd glimpsed when he'd removed his hat to shake off the raindrops reminded her of rich, dark chocolate. She hadn't dared check out the rest of his body. Dangerous territory, she decided. Dangerous and delicious.

Just the thought of food had her stomach rumbling in a most unladylike manner. Lately, it seemed she was constantly hungry. Who knew carrying twins would make her so ravenous? And cranky. Really cranky, according to Wes and Hutch. Remembering how rude she'd been after her rescue today, she was surprised the man hadn't driven off and left her standing in the rain. After all, he'd only been trying to help. And Hercules *had* been pretty scary.

She held back a sigh. She wasn't a bad person. Not really. What was it about her life that constantly made her responsible for everyone else's welfare? First, her mother's, and now this broken-down ranch with two geriatric ranch hands, not to mention her swiftly approaching introduction to Motherhood 101.

Parenting was something she'd never expected to deal with and she doubted she'd ever make a competent rancher, either, but she was darn well going to give both ventures her best shot. Nobody could call Gracie Castle a quitter.

The rain changed into a light drizzle as Whit guided the pickup down the black ribbon of wet pavement at a steady five miles over the legal limit. Gracie was tempted to ask him to drive a little faster. Another darn reminder of her pregnancy was the need for frequent trips to the bathroom. She crossed her legs and tried not to squirm.

Minutes later, two towering oak trees came into view, standing guard on either side of a graveled drive. Gracie breathed a sigh of relief.

"Turn there." She pointed to the sign over the drive. "That's it, the Castle Ranch. Don't be fooled by the name, though. The place isn't even close to a real castle."

A strangled cough came from the cowboy as they passed under the iron archway displaying the ranch's name and its crowned C brand, bumping and rattling over the iron cattle guard. "Sorry for the rough ride," he said, stopping the truck when they reached the building.

The ranch house was a long, low building shaped like a shoebox that had sprouted tentacles on each side. Wes had told Gracie the additions were added through the years as the family's needs grew. Now the homestead stood bleak and in need of much repair. With the emphasis on *much*, Gracie said to herself.

"This is your place? The Castle ranch?"

The surprised look on the man's face lasted only a moment, but long enough for Gracie to catch it. To his credit, he made no snide remarks about the name.

"Yes," she answered, thankful he didn't ask for further explanation. "You can let me out here."

She opened the door and got out of the truck without waiting for Whit's help. The rain had stopped too late to matter and she was already soaked to her skin. She might be big as a hippopotamus, but she didn't need sympathy. She really didn't care to make a bigger spectacle of herself than she'd already done.

A dozen squawking chickens flapped off the porch rail in a feathered frenzy as she approached the porch. Gracie took one look at their mess and stifled the sudden urge to scream. Wes had promised he'd wash off the porch while she was gone. He probably thought the rain would do it for him. When would she learn to just do the darned chores herself? She hated chickens.

She really did.

"Crazy birds." She stepped over a muddy puddle, carefully dodging other, less desirable obstacles in the yard. Not that her shoes would know the difference now.

When she realized Whit was following her onto the porch, she called out a warning. "Watch where you step." Maybe he needed a job, after all. No, she decided. He was probably just curious.

What were her resident bunkhouse boys going to say about this latest problem with Clementine? They'd already made it clear her cooking ability exceeded her knowledge of ranching chores. They might be right about that, but she knew when things needed cleaning. And the porch definitely was in need.

She didn't look forward to confessing she'd failed to bring Clementine home. Wes and Hutch had stubbornly argued with her over her decision to go after Clementine alone. They made their opinions loud and clear. She'd never be able to handle the job. When they'd put their heads together to figure out a way to do it themselves, she immediately invoked her power as ranch owner and vetoed their suggestions. She couldn't afford for either of them to get hurt. She already had more problems than she could handle. She didn't need the added responsibility of two injured old men requiring nursing care. Not to mention the perplexing brand-new problem standing right next to her, waiting to be invited inside.

She sighed and reached for the door. Whoever her cowboy rescuer was, he deserved a chance to dry off.

"Come on in, Mr. Carter. I'll get a towel for you."

Whit opened the door to let her enter first. "Thank you, ma'am. And you can call me Whit. I'll just wait here."

"Oh, don't worry about the floor." She headed off down the hall. "A little water won't hurt it." Do it good, she thought.

Gracie smiled at his concern for the worn, planked floors. His gentlemanly gesture of opening the door for her boosted her opinion of him up a notch, too.

The large, old-fashioned kitchen was the biggest room in the house and the one needing the most repairs. Gracie skirted the metal bucket sitting in the middle of the room the way she'd done every day for the last week and pointed to the water-stained ceiling. "Leaks," she said, as if he couldn't figure that out all by himself.

She dug a hand towel from a drawer by the old-fashioned galvanized sink and handed it to Whit. "Please excuse me for a minute while I get changed. There's fresh coffee made. Help yourself if you'd like." She pointed to an automatic coffee maker on the counter.

Her sense of propriety and good manners kicked in once she was back in her own territory. The idea of offering the stranger a job still hovered in the back of her mind. She seriously considered it when he took off his hat and rubbed his hair dry. Fantasizing images of him pitching hay under the hot Texas sun made concentration almost impossible. Of course, she didn't even know if she owned any hay fields, but if she did . . . .

"Some coffee would be great, if it's not too much trouble." Gracie blinked, regrouped her thoughts. "Oh, no trouble. I always have coffee made since I never know when Wes and Hutch will show up." She excused herself and hurried out of the room.

In her absence, Whit took the opportunity to examine his surroundings. The old kitchen was large and airy, thanks to wide windows on the east and west walls. The *plink-plink* of water hitting the bottom of the bucket confirmed her comment about the leaky roof and he wondered what else needed repairs. Gracie had warned him the name Castle didn't reflect the actual condition of the place. She was sure right about that. The whole place looked like it hadn't been maintained properly for several years.

Still, the room held a homey atmosphere that spoke of a lifetime of family gatherings, hearty ranch cooking, laughter and possibly, some tears. A life style Whit had longed for as a kid, but only experienced during those few summers spent at his maternal grandparents' small ranch. Thinking of Pop and Gram brought a smile to his face along with a bittersweet sadness. He still missed them.

A tall, glass-fronted pine cabinet along the opposite wall from where he sat caught his attention. Shelf after shelf held finely painted china tea cups and saucers, so delicate Whit knew they would probably bring a good price at an antique auction. Pretty fancy stuff for what appeared to be an ordinary ranch fallen on hard times.

The rest of the room showed no signs of any recent updating. Planked wood floors, boot-scuffed from years of ranch hands coming and going, were rough and in need of sanding and polishing. The windows were framed by clean, but lifeless red and white checked curtains, faded and streaked from the unforgiving rays of the Texas sun. Had Gracie been the one to add the domestic touches to the room?

A heavy wooden trestle-style table occupied the center of the room. The clear glass vase held a sparse bouquet of wildflowers, mostly daisies.

The apparent effort to brighten up the place only accentuated the lack of modern, efficient appliances. The Castle Ranch was definitely having hard times, Whit decided. And that was going to make his job even easier.

He was standing by the sink, looking out the window toward the outbuildings when Gracie walked in.

"You haven't helped yourself to coffee yet," she said.

"Why don't you sit down and let me pour some for both of us?" he asked, and pulled a chair out from the table for her. "You should be taking it easy."

He waited for her to sit, then filled two thick, white mugs with dark, fragrant coffee and handed one to her.

Strangely enough, the Castle ranch had been his final destination when he left his father and brother in San Antonio. If he hadn't lingered in town after the meeting to pick out a new hat and buy an extra pair of boots, he'd have been here before the storm blew in. Now he was reluctant to leave.

He had a few pertinent questions for the ranch owner before he revealed his real business here. But first, he needed to find out exactly who owned the Castle land. According to the information he'd obtained from the company's research department, the owner was an elderly widow named Rose Castle. Those records were obviously incorrect. Out-dated, to say the least. The chance for conversation now was exactly what he'd hoped for.

"I owe you an apology," Gracie said quietly as she took the chair. "And a thank-you, too." She'd changed her clothes for dry ones, but her auburn curls were still damp.

"No apology needed," he said, taking a seat on the opposite side of the table. "I guess I wasn't exactly a gentleman back there, so I apologize for being a little rough. I didn't want to wait around to see whether or not that bull was a friendly Ferdinand type or the pasture's security guard."

He sampled the coffee and grinned. "Ahhh, just the way I like it, strong and hot. None of that fancy-flavored stuff for me."

Gracie favored him with a smile. "Well, I wasn't a waitress for nothing. Besides, Wes and Hutch gave me some pointers about cowboy coffee. I've never seen anyone as picky as those two."

Whit's chance to ask about the two men was cut short when the back screen door squeaked on its hinges and the subjects of the conversation tromped in, grumbling and shaking the rain from their hats.

"Here they are now," Gracie said, with a soft laugh. "They can smell fresh coffee a mile away."

The two men hung up their hats on the wall hooks by the door and immediately gave Whit a cautious, squint-eyed once over. Whit stood and offered his hand. The men remained where they were until Gracie spoke.

"Whit Carter, meet the oldest fixtures on the Castle ranch, Wes Paxton and Hutch Hutchinson, my inherited advisors in all ranching matters."

Whit stepped forward, hand still extended. "Glad to meet you, gentlemen."

Wes was the first to accept the handshake. "Carter, you say? Well, howdy. What brings you out in this gulley-washer?"

Whit hesitated just long enough to raise Hutch's eyebrows. "I happened along in time to help Gracie out of an . . . uh, unusual situation."

"What—?" Hutch shot a scowl Gracie's way. "Didn't we tell you fetching Clementine was no job for you to tackle in your condition? You shoulda' let us call somebody." He filled two cups from the coffee pot and handed one to Wes. Both men took a seat at the table, their gazes still fastened on Whit, though they spoke directly to Gracie.

Whit wondered who else was around to help. She'd already told him she had no husband or ranch hands, but the child she carried had to have a father somewhere. And if he wasn't, it was clear he should be.

Now it was Wes's turn to raise his eyebrows. "Where's Clementine? She didn't have her calf already, did she? Why didn't you holler for us when you brought her in?"

Both men looked to Gracie for answers as they drank their coffee, but Whit didn't miss the way the pair kept shooting glances his way. He knew *possessive* when he saw it, and these old codgers were full of it. They might not be physically strong, but Whit would bet good money they'd put up a fight with anyone who threatened Gracie. After meeting them, he understood why she wouldn't let them go after the heifer. The aging cowboys wouldn't stand a chance against that four-legged steamroller they called Hercules.

"Clementine's still out there," Gracie said. "Hercules wasn't too happy when Whit vaulted the fence to help me. We both got out just in time. Since it was raining so hard, Whit brought me home to get a cattle hauler for Clementine. We have one of those, don't we?"

"Well, uh," the men stammered in unison, clearly confused.

"If you two can round up a trailer of some sort, I have a ball hitch on my truck," Whit offered. "The heifer looked like she wasn't going to wait much longer to have that calf." He spoke directly to Wes and Hutch, stifling a grin when they perked up as soon as he asked for their help.

Gracie looked at the clock on the wall. "We've been back for more than half-an-hour. We have to go back for Clementine now." She sent a questioning look Whit's way.

Standing a bit straighter, the two older men nodded and set their coffee cups aside.

"You bet, young feller. I know just the thing that'll work," Wes said, puffing out his chest. "Git a move on, Hutch. We got us some work to do."

Hutch hustled out the door right behind Wes. "We'll be right back," he said over his shoulder.

Gracie's worried look prompted Whit to call after them. "Wait up. I'll go with you."

He took off in a lope, wondering where the old men were going to find a trailer among the rusty collection of old farm equipment he'd seen parked haphazardly behind the barn.

His first impression of the ranch was correct. There might be fancy tea cups in the china cabinet, but in reality, the Castle ranch was in financial straits, just as he'd expected. What he didn't understand, though, was where Gracie fit in the picture. He hoped her 'bunkhouse boys' would give him some answers when he got them alone.

The men stood over a small utility trailer obviously built before the Alamo existed. The sad-looking object couldn't possibly haul the heifer, or anything else, without falling apart. Loose floor boards and one flat tire proved that point.

Whit shook his head. "You aren't planning to actually use this, are you?"

"Sure thing," Wes said. "This here trailer's been hauling stock and fence rails ever since way before you cut your teeth, young feller. It'll haul Clementine just fine. A couple of new boards in the bottom and it'll be just like new." He turned to Hutch, who was already on the trailer throwing off a bunch of empty feed sacks and an accumulation of rusted tools. "Got some right over there." He pointed to a pile of weathered lumber. "Planned on using them for a new chicken coop, but the darned hens would rather stay on the porch. Hutch spoiled 'em after the boss lady died."

"Did not," Hutch retorted, bending over to pick up an old hammer and a bucket of nails. He handed them to Whit. "Here, see what you can do with these."

Whit took the tools and barely had time to set them down before Hutch's boot heel caught on a rough board. With a hoarse cry, the old cowboy fell smack into Whit's outstretched arms and both men landed on the ground with a thud.

"Ohhhh." The older man groaned and rolled over. Whit scrambled to his feet, taking care as he helped Hutch into a sitting position.

Wes hurried over to the pair. "Take it easy, old man," he said, concern evident in his trembling voice. "What're you trying to do, fly?"

"I'm fine," Hutch insisted, though Whit worried there might be more than just a rough board causing Hutch's fall.

"How many fingers do you see?" Whit held up his hand.

"I see five. Can't you count?"

Whit wasn't convinced. "Are you able to move your arm? Tell me your name. Do you know where you are?"

"Those are the dumbest questions I ever heard," Hutch grumbled. "All I done was stumble. Now help me up and let's go get that heifer 'fore she calves out there and we have two critters to haul."

Wes had been quiet during the other men's exchange, but the anxious look on his wrinkled face told Whit the man was frightened at the thought of his friend suffering an injury.

"I'm pretty sure he's all right," Whit assured Wes. "I think it would be a good idea if he stayed with Gracie, though, while you and I bring Clementine home."

Wes agreed, much to his friend's dismay.

"I told you I'm fine," Hutch insisted, shooting Wes a dirty look. But in the end, he lost the argument and Wes accompanied him to the house, leaving Whit to repair the trailer.

Forty-five minutes later, Whit and Wes headed for the pasture with the trailer bouncing behind the truck. The flat tire was pumped up, though Whit wouldn't guarantee its longevity. He just wanted to get this job done so he could be on his way.

Whit drove carefully, aware of the bouncing trailer he pulled. Wes worried out loud about the future of the ranch and Gracie's impending delivery date.

"Sounds like your employer's got herself in a real fix."

"You don't know the half of it," Wes said, motioning for Whit to stop the truck by the pasture gate so he could get out and open it.

There wasn't time for Whit to consider Wes's comment until after the heifer had been coaxed into the trailer and they were headed back to the ranch.

Curious about the ranch and its owner, Whit subtly tried to draw out more information from Wes, but the older man didn't offer any interesting tidbits other than Gracie needed to hire more hands.

From what he'd observed so far, Whit got the impression hiring more help wasn't financially possible. That made him all the more certain his offer to lease the property with option to buy would be accepted. As a ranch owner and soon-to-be single mom, Gracie would definitely need money. He wasn't unsympathetic to the woman's plight, but she obviously hadn't stopped to consider the consequences of her actions with the father of her unborn child. Safe sex wasn't a new invention, for cryin' out loud. The kids were always the ones that were short-changed in a situation like this. His own family situation was different, but just as painful.

Stop jumping to conclusions, he reprimanded himself. Somewhere, there might be a daddy who truly did care. Still, if that was true, you'd think the man would make a point to be around to take care of his family's needs. If you didn't want to pay, you'd better not play.

Whit shrugged. Hell, he had no business making judgment. What did he know about family needs? The Lovett clan had been dysfunctional since the beginning of time. That was the very reason Whit had decided to remain single and childless

Chapter Three

Gracie walked to the front window and looked down the road for the umpteenth time since the two men left, then joined Hutch on the front porch. He sat in a green plastic lawn chair, bemoaning his plight in a gruff voice in between gulps of the iced tea Gracie brought him.

"I shoulda' gone with them. They'll need extra hands. We sure could use more help around here."

Gracie pulled up another chair, blew off a few remaining feathers and sat down next to Hutch. "I agree, but there doesn't seem to be anyone looking for work around here. Not for what I can afford to pay, anyway. Truthfully, I don't know what to do next, Hutch. Do you think Clementine will be all right?" Her own approaching delivery date was drawing closer and with each passing day Gracie grew more apprehensive about the situation facing her.

Hutch shrugged. "I 'spect she'll do fine. She's young and healthy. And if there's a problem, that cowboy you found seems capable of handling things." He rubbed his whiskered chin. "I wonder where he's headed. We could sure use somebody like him around here."

"I already asked him if he wanted a job. He said he wasn't looking for work."

Hutch emptied his glass in one last swallow and set it down. "Too bad. He looked like a hard worker. Maybe you oughta' ask him again when they get back."

That possibility had already crossed Gracie's mind. More than once.

The rattle of the truck and trailer broke through Gracie's deep thoughts. She went inside to change into her barn boots before making her way through the muddy path to the barn. Hutch had already hobbled out there and was watching the men unload the unhappy heifer.

Clementine must have known she was home because she didn't waste any time walking off the ramp and into the barn. Wes led her to a stall already covered in clean straw bedding. The tired animal was more than ready to lie down.

Limping slightly, Hutch brought a pail of water, but by that time the mama-to-be was in the throes of labor.

"Do something," Gracie pleaded, looking at Whit.

"Hey, don't look at me," he said, backing away. "Never delivered a calf before in my life. Wes? Hutch? You boys are probably old hands at this, right?"

Wes shook his head. "Been a long time. We ain't got the strength we useta' have. But we can tell you how it goes. I don't think Clementine here will have any trouble, even though this is her first one. C'mon over here." He motioned for Whit to join him at the heifer's side. "The main thing is that the front feet and head have to come first. If they don't, then we got trouble. Most times, the mama does all the work herself."

Whit swallowed hard. "Well, let's hope this mama knows the rules."

Gracie thought the man looked a trifle uneasy for a true cowboy, but just then Wes shouted and all heck broke loose. There wasn't time for any more questions.

Hutch pushed Whit closer, but Gracie hung back. The fact that she was witnessing an actual birth was an awesome sight. She was scared, yet filled with wonder at the same time.

Everything happened so fast, Gracie barely had time to register what was taking place. The newborn slipped from the safety of its mother's body feet and head first and Clementine took over the business of tending her baby as if she'd done it a dozen times.

Gracie watched, fascinated, while the new mama cleaned her newborn, making sure everything was as it should be. The animal's instinctive maternal reaction snagged at something softly sentimental in Gracie's heart. She prayed she'd have the same instinct when her time came.

When the wobbly youngster finally struggled to stand on legs that weren't quite ready, Whit was there to help. In no time, he had the calf nuzzling its mama and Clementine settled down to the matter of taking care of her brand-new son. Gracie knew right then she wanted to give her babies a place to belong. Was it possible she'd found that place here at the Castle ranch?

She wasn't quite sure how she was going to thank this stranger for his help. Whit Carter was definitely no ordinary cowboy. Her heart had stumbled a tiny bit at the gentle way he helped the new calf learn how to nurse from its mother. Gracie refused to believe Whit's sexy, dark looks might be the cause of her heart-fluttering sensations.

Ridiculous thoughts, she chided herself. You're pregnant and definitely don't need a man in your life. Of course, if he was looking for a job, she'd hire him in a minute. Since Whit had already said NO to that possibility, she had to find an alternative.

When she arrived here from Minneapolis, Gracie learned from Wes that Rose Castle had kept the ranch from totally failing by charging a fee for the prize bull's service. Gracie discovered when she went over the ledgers that for months before her grandmother's death, there'd hardly been enough demand for that to keep the accounts in the black. Hercules was barely earning his keep. That would have to change. But how? She didn't have a clue where to begin.

The old men explained about A-I, the new way of breeding used by most ranchers now that required more knowledge and equipment than Rose had been able to acquire. Not many ranchers wanted to actually rent a breeding bull when obtaining the semen by artificial insemination was easier, quicker, and safer for the heifer or cow. Sadly, Rose hadn't been able to keep up with progress. This new bull calf was the last of Hercules' progeny.

That kind of talk had given Gracie a headache. She knew nothing about breeding animals and truly didn't want to learn.

And thinking about the ledgers reminded her she needed to finish that tedious task before Whit left. Wes and Hutch had already assured her they could look after Clementine and little Junior, but she'd be easier knowing Whit was still in the barn with them.

Before she left the barn, Gracie made the pair promise to call her if they needed help. For what, she had no idea, but she didn't want either one of them getting hurt by doing something foolish. There wasn't enough money for hospital bills right now. She was grateful Hutch only had a few bruises and sore muscles from his fall. She worried about him, now more than ever.

Still searching her mind for a way to thank Whit, she wished there were funds enough to pay him in cash, though something told her he would refuse her offer. She entered the kitchen and made her way down the hall to what used to be her grandmother's office and took a seat behind the finely carved oak desk.

A smell of old leather and a faint scent of lavender greeted her when she entered the room. She suspected the flowery fragrance had been her grandmother's favorite. She'd seen an empty crystal perfume bottle on the dark wood vanity in the front bedroom, where the scent of lavender still lingered. Gracie tried to imagine Rose Castle standing at the mirror checking her image before taking on the rigors of running the ranch. Did she wear pants or skirts? Was she tall or short? Temperamental or soft-spoken? There was so much she didn't know about her grandmother. So much her mother had chosen to keep from her. And what about her grandfather? Those two old timers out there in the barn were experts at sealing their lips whenever she approached that particular subject.

A hesitant knock at the door brought her out of her reverie. She looked up from her place behind her grandmother's desk. Whit stood in the doorway, hat in hand. His crooked smile sent a shamelessly good feeling skittering down Gracie's nervous system. Indecently good, she admitted when her heart bumped into her ribs. "Yes?" she finally managed when her breathing slowed.

"I've reconsidered your offer," he said. "That is, if the job's still open."

Gracie rounded the desk, so grateful for whatever caused Whit's change of plans she could've hugged him. Thank goodness she stopped just in time to keep from embarrassing herself, but not before she caught a brief flash of something dangerous in Whit's dark eyes.

They stood mere inches apart. His nearness caused a sudden, delicious warmth to spread through Gracie's body. The way her pulse pounded at the outrageous thoughts spinning in her head shocked her. Good grief, was she attracted to him? Afraid he could see the flush in her face, she quickly stepped back and composed herself.

"That's wonderful," she said, breathlessly. "When can you start? I'll have Wes and Hutch fix a place for you in the bunkhouse."

Whit looked disconcerted for a moment, but when her questioning gaze met his, he quickly averted his eyes.

"Well, I have a couple of matters to take care of first. I can be back here by the first of next week," he said. "That okay with you?"

Gracie nodded. Did he think she would argue? He hadn't even asked about wages.

"The job doesn't pay much," she told him, carefully watching his reaction, "but meals are included, as well as laundry facilities." She named the amount she had calculated she could afford to pay and held her breath. He didn't even flinch. Gracie's spirits soared.

"Sounds fair to me," Whit said, settling his hat on his head. "I'll see you next week, then. And thanks." He touched the brim of the Stetson.

"No, thank *you*, Mr. Carter," Gracie insisted as she followed him to the front door.

He turned back, a glint in his coffee-dark eyes. "Just Whit will do," he said and moseyed down the steps.

She struggled to keep from jumping up and down as she watched him walk off the porch and out to his truck. Not that she could jump with her belly so big. The excitement of hiring her first ranch hand bubbled up inside her. Now she had a cowboy of her own. In a manner of speaking, of course. Just wait until she told Wes and Hutch. And they thought she'd never be a competent rancher. Humph! She'd show them. She waited until Whit's truck sped off down the road, then hurried to tell the men her good news. Oh, she had a thousand things to do before the new hired hand returned.

Walking way too fast, she reached the bunkhouse and screamed. The sharp pain she'd been ignoring grabbed hold of her like a massive vise. She was doubled over, moaning and holding her stomach when Wes opened the door. She pitched forward and he caught her just before she collapsed in his arms.

"Hutch, get on out here and help me!" The startled old cowboy did his best to hold on to her until Hutch came hobbling in from the back of the building.

"Here, young lady, see if you can sit down," Hutch said as the pair helped her to the only chair inside the sparsely-furnished room.

Gracie panted, breathing like she'd been instructed in her Lamaze class. "I'm . . . all right, I think." She managed to sit up when the pain subsided. "I don't know what happened. I felt fine, then all at once, BAM! Never mind, I'm better now." The anxious look on the men's faces tugged at her heart. To think they cared touched her deeply. "Sorry to be such a problem."

"Don't you worry none about that, missy," Wes told her. "Me an' Hutch will look after you. You just sit there until you feel like going back to the big house. Ain't no hurry."

"What were you coming out here for?" Hutch stood by her chair, his gnarled hands shaking slightly as he patted her shoulder. "Did you need us for somethin'?"

Gracie brightened, remembering the good news she had for the men. "Oh, I almost forgot. Mr. Carter, uh, I mean Whit, changed his mind. He's going to take the job, after all. And he agreed to start next week. Isn't that wonderful?" She looked from one man to the other, waiting for their approval.

Wes was the first to speak, as usual. "You don't say. Well now, I reckon we'll have to fix him up with a place to stay. That spare room at the back of the bunkhouse ought to be okay. 'Course, it'll need a good cleaning. Or did you have a mind to let him stay in the big house?"

Gracie felt her face flush. "Of course not! What a crazy idea. Shame on you, Wes. You know I'd never do that."

Hutch scowled. "Yeah, Wes, what's the matter with your head? Gracie ain't like that."

"Well, I saw how they stared at each other," the man said. "Even with her being pregnant and all, the man couldn't keep his eyes off her. Hell, I know when a man's got ideas in his head. I'm old, but I ain't dead."

Gracie had to smile at the thought of Wes as a young man with ideas. But she didn't think she provoked any such ideas in Whit Carter's head. Not the way she looked right now. And if he *was* looking at her, he was probably trying to figure out how she could possibly hope to keep the ranch solvent with only a bull and a couple of cows. She wished she had an answer.

"Enough talk," Gracie scolded. "I can make it back to the house now." Why the pair kept referring to the main house as *big* was beyond her. The place was nothing but an odd stretch of old rooms in need of major repair. With a leaky roof. And a porch full of chickens that needed painting. Not the chickens, just the porch.

She started to get up. The men stood on either side of her each awkwardly taking one of her arms. "I can make it by myself," she said louder, thinking it might be safer if she did.

When she realized no amount of arguing would change the oldster's minds, she gave in and let them help her back to the house. That was easier than arguing. Well, not really.

They walked slowly, each man holding tightly to her arms, making it difficult to walk three abreast on the narrow path. When they reached the back door to the kitchen, the men jostled for space, finally getting her inside without pulling her arms out of their sockets.

Wes insisted she rest in bed for the remainder of the afternoon. The idea of resting undisturbed was certainly appealing, but Gracie didn't want to spend the whole day isolated in her bedroom.

"Just let me lie down on the living room sofa for a little while," she said. "I'll be all right in a few minutes." *Please let that be true,* she begged silently, exhaustion suddenly overcoming her.

The men spread a blanket on the sofa for her, fussing over her and making sure she was comfortable. They waited until she closed her eyes before retreating to the kitchen.

Gracie dozed off listening to their hushed whispers. A short time later, she woke up with the mother of all backaches gripping her and a very wet spot on the blanket underneath her.

"Oh-my-gosh! Wes! Hutch!" She tried to sit up but changed her mind when the shooting pain intensified. *Dear God, don't let this be the babies. Not now.* "Wes!" she called again. Where were they?

The men came running as fast as their arthritic legs would let them. "What's wrong?" they shouted in unison, bumping into each other as they ran.

Wes took one look at the situation and said, "Hutch, old man, we got us another delivery on our hands."

Hutch paled. "I'll go call the doc." He started out of the room but stopped in the doorway. "Wait. Who do I call? I don't know any doctor except the veterinarian."

"Well, call him then," Wes yelled. "Now go!" He turned to Gracie after Hutch left the room. "Now then, young lady, you and me are gonna have a talk." He pulled a foot stool over beside the sofa and sat, taking Gracie's soft hand in his rough one.

"If for some reason these little ones decide to make an appearance before we get some help, it'll be up to the three of us to see that they get here without any problems, understand? I promise me 'n Hutch will take good care of you." He took a watch out of his pocket and noted the time. "You just try to relax."

Easy for him to say, Gracie thought as the ache intensified. She knew Wes was trying to comfort her and that alone gave her hope that everything would be all right. When another low pain gripped her back, she knew the doctor wasn't going to arrive in time. The only thing she could do now was pray the old cowboys would be able to help her. Tears welled up in her eyes as she suddenly grasped the enormity of the circumstance. This wasn't how she envisioned the birth would be when she agreed to become a surrogate mother. Not even close. Nothing was turning out the way she'd planned.

Hutch came barreling back into the room, his face whiter than it had been earlier, if that was possible. "Doc Turner said he'd call another doctor who was closer to the ranch. Said to get blankets and sheets and . . . I don't remember what else he said."

Shamefaced, he handed the sheets to Wes and backed away from the sofa, clearly uncomfortable with the situation. "I can't find the blankets."

If she hadn't been in such pain, Gracie would have tried to reassure the worried man, but all she could do was grit her teeth and try not to cry out. *Oh God, please help us all.* She'd handle the labor pains as long as the babies were safe. She wasn't sure about Wes and Hutch.

A sharp knock at the front door interrupted her thoughts.

"How about that? The other doc must've been right down the road," Hutch said and hurried to let him in while Wes slipped the dry sheets under Gracie.

Hutch yanked open the front door. "Well, I'll be! You ain't the doc, but come on in, 'cause we need all the help we can get."

Whit Lovett walked into the house in time to hear Gracie's next heart-wrenching cry. "Tell the doctor to hurry. Please!"

Chapter Four

If ever Whit wanted to be somewhere else, this was the moment. And if he had any sense, he'd turn around and run. Seeing Gracie in such distress when he walked through the door wasn't what he expected when he'd returned to the ranch to leave his cell phone number with her, in case she needed to get in touch with him before next week. Now he wished he'd kept on driving.

Ice cold fear tied his gut in a knot as he watched Wes wipe Gracie's face with a moist cloth, all the time murmuring quiet words of encouragement to her. Even Hutch seemed to know what to do. Whit had never felt as helpless as he did right then. Warily, he approached the sofa and knelt beside Wes. The older man nodded and handed the cloth to Whit.

"Here," Wes said. "You take over while I go see what's keeping the doctor. Think you can keep her comfortable until I get back?" He gave Whit's shoulder an assuring squeeze. Whit nodded with a confidence he damn sure didn't feel.

Wes was slow to rise from his kneeling position before he turned to Hutch. "See if you can find some more sheets or blankets. The doc will need something to wrap around the baby, I 'spect."

Both men left the room, Wes giving Hutch more instructions and Hutch muttering, "Yep, yep, okay."

Never had Whit felt so inadequate. He could negotiate a profitable land lease deal with no problem, but what he knew about assisting a birth wouldn't fill one of those fancy tea cups he'd seen in that old china cabinet in the kitchen. Granted, he did okay with Clementine, but this was a totally different matter. Totally. This was a woman. And one he didn't know very well, at that. One that should've known better than to go chasing heifers in a rainstorm. Hell, he didn't want to be Mr. Midwife!

He moved the moist cloth across her face, wiping away the perspiration and a few tears. Gracie looked up at him through tear-dampened lashes and right then, Whit thought she was the most beautiful woman he'd ever seen, in spite of her condition. Or maybe because of it. Either way, he wanted to help her but didn't have a clue as to what she needed.

"What can I do, Gracie? How can I help?" He felt like a gate-crasher at a very private party.

Gracie licked her dry lips and shook her head. "Could you help me to my bedroom and stay with me until the doctor gets here. Please?" More tears leaked from the corners of her eyes. Whit dabbed them away, then took Gracie's hands and hooked them behind his neck.

"Hold on," he said, scooping her up and heading for the bedroom. "Don't worry, I'll stay with you." The least he could do was reassure her she wouldn't have to go through this alone. He tore his gaze away from her trembling lips, ashamed that he still felt the cowardly urge to run.

Gracie smiled a wobbly smile. "I thought you'd already left the ranch."

"Had to come back. Forgot to give you my cell phone number in case you needed to contact me. Sure didn't expect that to happen this soon." He squeezed her hands and felt her squeeze back when another contraction swamped her.

"Shouldn't we be timing these or something?"

"Don't worry, I am." Wes strode into the bedroom behind them, holding up his watch. "Doc's on another call but he'll be here shortly. Said to call 9—1-1 now, just in case he's late. Hang in there, Gracie."

"He'd . . . better get here . . . soon," Gracie gasped.

"Yeah, very soon," Whit muttered under his breath. Right now, he felt about as useful as ice cube trays in hell.

Then everything started happening at once.

"Call now!" Gracie yelled. She grabbed a handful of Whit's shirt, pulled his panic-stricken face close to hers and whispered a very detailed explanation of the situation and what she needed him to do.

With only the length of her eyelashes separating them, Gracie watched as the shock in Whit's dark eyes softened to concern.

"Aw, hell, Gracie." He brushed her perspiring forehead with a gentle touch. "I didn't know about that part."

In that emotion-packed moment, Gracie's heart somersaulted. What on earth . . .? Her pregnancy hormones must be flying off the charts. Before she could put her reaction to Whit's look into perspective, another contraction seized her. "Call, I said!"

Whit fumbled for his phone, dropping it when she tightened her hold on his shirt front.

"And put it on speaker so I can hear, too," she demanded as wave after wave of unrelenting pain washed over her. "Do I have to tell you everything? Wes, go make coffee or something. Take Hutch with you and stay in there, both of you!"

The pair scooted out of the room. Whit's eyes widened. "Where are you going? I might need you!" He scrambled around on the floor looking for his phone.

Static garbled the operator's voice when Whit finally found it. He pressed the Speaker button and shouted into it. "Babies! She's having babies!" He tossed the phone on the nightstand

"All right, sir," the emergency operator said. "Y'all just stay calm, you hear? Can you tell me your location?"

Gracie screeched the directions to the ranch and Whit repeated them.

"Don't worry now, medics are on the way," he calm, motherly voice drawled. "Now, listen carefully, young man. Here's what you're gonna' do . . ." The operator's instructions were vividly graphic.

Whit panicked. "I can't do that! I'm no doctor!"

"You have to!" Gracie really wanted to hit something with both fists. "It's not supposed to happen this way," she cried.

Whit shot the hysterical about-to-be-mom a harried look from the foot of the bed and pointed toward the action taking place there. "Hell, don't tell me, tell them!"

"Just pay attention," Gracie shouted back.

Whit ignored her. "There's two of them, you know," he yelled into the phone. "Two!"

"Yes, I know, sir," the operator said. "Just stay calm. Y'all are doing fine. Now, can you . . . ?"

Gracie didn't hear the rest of what the operator said. She was too busy focusing all her energy on one final, scream-like-a-banshee-swear-like-a-sailor push.

With his heart pounding like a tom-tom, Whit caught the tiny newborn in his trembling hands. His insides went all soft and mushy as an astounding warmth filled every corner of his normally indifferent heart.

"Oh. Oh, thank God, Oooh." Gracie's quiet sobs were mixed with nervous laughter. "Is everything all right? Girl or boy? Let me see. Oh, hurry!"

Whit barely managed a hoarse "Yes. Girl." He was too busy concentrating on the rest of the operator's instructions and trying not to pass out. He was delivering babies, for cryin' out loud. Totally unbelievable. Love at first sight of this tiny person had gobsmacked him. He was a goner. No doubt about it.

Knees still shaking, he laid the towel-wrapped babe on Gracie's tummy. Another unfamiliar emotion snatched the breath from his tight chest, forcing him to turn away when unexpected dampness blurred his vision. Well, hell.

Then Gracie yelled at him again and he was back in action just in time to welcome the second baby, a dark-haired little boy. Whit Carter Lovett the Third lost his heart for the second time that day.

"One of each," he whispered, overwhelmed by the moment and the miracle. "You've got one of each." A wave of tenderness the size of Texas filled his chest, making it damn near impossible to speak. The sheer wonder of delivering two tiny human beings into the world shook him right down to his hand-tooled boots.

Exhilarated and totally awestruck, he was more than happy to relinquish his position at the foot of the bed when the medics came rushing into the room. He would never do this again. Never. If he stopped to think about the past frantic moments, hell, he'd keel over. When he looked at the infants snuggled in their mama's loving arms, his insides went all mushy again, as if he was somehow connected to all of them.

Gracie shifted one of the babies to her side and reached out for Whit's hand. Her whispered, teary-eyed, "Thanks, cowboy," was all it took to make him smile and give her hand a squeeze. The lump in his throat was suddenly the size of a tumbleweed and just as scratchy. Aw, hell.

Whit had moved aside to make room for the medics just as someone claiming to be a doctor burst through the door, pulled on surgical gloves and began shouting orders to the medics as he assessed the situation. Gracie whimpered again. Wes and Hutch had left the kitchen and were watching the excitement from the bedroom doorway. Whit knelt at Gracie's side, still holding her hand. Still wanting to run, even though the main event was under control now.

Someone shut his phone off. Someone else worked with the doctor when he cut the babies' cords and tended to Gracie. Another medic took charge of readying the gurney for transporting the trio.

When the physician finished, he smiled at Gracie and her newborns. "You did just fine, my dear. Two healthy babies." Then he turned to Whit. "Congratulations on your beautiful children."

Whit opened his mouth to explain but Gracie squeezed his hand so hard he was positive she'd cut off the circulation. So he just said "Thanks," and let it go at that for the moment.

Gracie looked at Whit with pleading, misty-green eyes. "I agree, they're the most beautiful babies in the world. You can see how much we need you." Then she focused her attention on the two reasons for all the excitement.

Whit focused on not passing out.

The doctor gave directions for the medics to prepare for transferring Gracie and the twins to the local hospital while he jotted down pertinent notes in a folder full of scribbled on pages.

Whit relaxed, the mention of his role as the twins' father evidently forgotten by the doctor.

Gracie wept silent tears of joy and relief. Whit almost did the same, not for joy, but because he was relieved the ordeal was over. He wouldn't have lasted much longer.

For as long as he lived, he would never forget the miracle he'd just witnessed or the strength Gracie had displayed. An uncomfortable feeling of inadequacy, more like weakness, nipped at his conscience. He wasn't a coward, but he was sure thankful men weren't expected to have babies. Admiration for this woman he barely knew caught him off-guard.

The babies made little mewling sounds while the medics assisted the good doctor in preparing Gracie and the newborns for their ambulance ride to the hospital.

All the while, two crusty old cowboys wiped their eyes and a cynical new ranch hand kept swallowing to keep his stomach in place. All three stood quietly taking in the whole unbelievable scenario.

Gracie teared up some after she'd held the twins, but they were tears of happiness when she saw for herself her new son and daughter were all right.

Whit leaned over and gently thumbed her tears away, surprised at the tug of tenderness this woman evoked in his carefully guarded emotions. He already felt an unexplained connection here since he'd played Mr. Midwife in the extraordinary event. Who knew the act of bringing the tiny twins into this world could cause such strange sensations in the area of his heart? He almost wished . . . .

No time for crazy thoughts. He pushed them away and focused on Gracie. "Hey, don't be crying. The doctor said everything went just fine. Try to rest now. They'll be taking you and the little ones to the hospital in a few minutes." His voice cracked ever so slightly as he spoke. He was uncomfortable with this type of situation and guessed Gracie was, too. Her strength during the ordeal amazed him. He was pretty sure being assisted by a total stranger while she gave birth to twins was a less than ideal situation, but she'd been a real trooper. And he really didn't mind her yelling at him. Much.

By the time the medics had Gracie and her babies ready for the ride to the hospital, the storm had subsided, leaving a damp chill in the air. Blankets were tucked around the new mama and the twins before they left the house.

Walking beside the gurney on the way to the ambulance, Whit held on to Gracie's hand. Letting her go alone never occurred to him.

"I hate to ask any more favors, Whit," Gracie said as the medics rolled the gurney up to the back of the rescue unit, "but could you possible stick around the ranch tonight, just in case Wes and Hutch need help with anything? I'm afraid all the excitement might have upset them." Anxious eyes and soft lips pleaded her cause, robbing Whit of what little good sense he had left. How could he refuse?

"Count on it," he said and leaned down to place a quick peck on her cheek. Just to reassure her, of course, he told his conscience. Nothing more.

As he stood watching the ambulance fade out of sight, his conscience questioned his true intentions. Too tired to figure that out at the moment, he turned and trudged back to the house. The adrenalin rush that had carried him through earlier took a sudden nose dive. But resting would have to wait. He still had Wes and Hutch waiting with questions he wasn't ready to answer yet and that kept his nerves jangled. Emotions he'd never experienced swirled through him, but he put aside thinking about them too closely until he had more time. Right now, there was plenty of work to occupy his mind.

Back in the house, he rolled up his sleeves and tackled the job of putting the house back in order. He was grateful to find Wes and Hutch already involved in the cleanup. The sooner they finished, the sooner he could get to the hospital.

As if he'd read Whit's mind, Hutch looked across the kitchen at the new hired hand. "You planning on heading for the hospital pretty soon?"

The older cowboy had just finished the load of laundry he'd tossed in the washer earlier during the confusion and was folding the clean sheets on the kitchen table while Whit washed dishes.

"Thought I would," Whit said, keeping his attention on the sink full of soapy water. "I told Gracie I'd look after things here first. You know, make sure the chores were done and all. Then I'll go to the hospital for a while. See how she's doing. You know."

"Hhmmph! Thought you had business to take care of somewhere. Weren't expecting you back until next week." Wes came in from the living room where he'd been putting things back in order.

Whit cleared his throat and kept washing dishes. "Yeah, well, that can wait until later," he said. "Gracie seemed to think it was important for me to stay tonight." When Wes glared at him, he quickly added, "That is, if it's all right with the two of you."

The last thing he wanted was for the men to get their feathers ruffled over his position as the new top hand. He'd need to stay on their good side if he wanted to find out the answers to his questions about the Castles. He also had to convince them he knew how to manage a ranch. He wasn't sure just yet how he was going to accomplish that feat, but he'd figure it out somehow.

How hard could it be? He'd have a bigger problem avoiding contact with his father and brother.

The pair nodded in unison. "Sure, Whit," Wes said. "Always plenty of work to do around here. More'n Gracie can handle. You know, me and Hutch ain't much help with the heavy jobs no more." This last admission was made with his head bowed.

"I'll help all I can," Whit assured the pair. "Just show me what to do."

Whit had managed a lot of projects in his career, but the only time he'd ever been around ranch animals was during his summer visits to his maternal grandparents place. Their small ranch near Kerrville was home to a small herd of black Angus cattle and a couple of docile horses. A younger Whit had loved riding with his grandfather. That had been years ago.

Back then, his teenage interests weren't exactly on work, but he remembered his grandfather as a hard-working man with genuine respect for his land. His white-haired grandmother was the perfect embodiment of every kid's imagination with a kitchen always filled with the tantalizing aromas of fresh-baked bread and sugar cookies. She smelled like cinnamon and vanilla when she hugged him tight in her loving arms. It was a scent he'd never forgotten. One he'd never experienced again since her death.

Over the years, Whit wondered what his own life would've been like if his father had been an ordinary rancher instead of the heir to a multi-million dollar company. He couldn't quite picture his mother wearing an apron and cooking meals in the kitchen. She was too fond of showing off her newest diamonds to the country club crowd.

Meantime, the experience on the Castle Ranch already had an interesting start. If everything turned out the way he hoped, he'd have the lease agreement for the Castle Ranch acreage locked in and LGS could begin the necessary underground surveying for geothermal resources. Gracie and her twins would have a tidy income every month to make their life a little easier and Whit could be on his way to West Texas or Wyoming and a new life. Yeah, a win-win situation. There was nothing keeping him in Texas.

He let the water out of the sink and dried his hands. He'd been waiting for an opening like this. A chance to ask some questions about Gracie and how she came to inherit the ranch. He pulled out a chair and sat down at the kitchen table.

Hutch picked up the sheets he'd finished folding and left the room. Wes tossed a dirty rag in the trash, washed his hands and sat down across from Whit with a cup of coffee.

"Got something bothering you, young feller?" Wes eyed Whit over the rim of his cup. He blew on his coffee, then sipped loudly.

"Matter of fact, I have," Whit admitted. "What's the scoop on Gracie and this ranch? I mean, where's her husband, the babies' father? And why isn't there more help around here? This is a good-sized spread."

Hutch had returned and sat drumming his knobby fingers on the table. "You sure got a lot of questions."

"Uh-huh." Whit waited, ready to accept the fact that getting answers from her bunkhouse boys was like trying to get water from a dry creek.

Wes looked Whit straight in the eye. "The father's dead."

"Oh, she's a widow, then?" That explained a lot.

"Nope, there never was a husband, either. Not Gracie's, anyway. Ya' see, she was having those babies for another couple. A surrogate mom thing, she told us. But the real parents got themselves killed in a boating accident right after Gracie got pregnant. So now the babies are Gracie's responsibility."

For the second time that day, Whit realized his mouth was hanging open. Was there no end to the surprises around here? The thought of Gracie having kids for someone else didn't seem right, although he knew it happened more often than the news media reported. He wasn't sure why that bothered him, but it did. That was something he intended to figure out right after he took care of the business that brought him to the Castle ranch in the first place. As soon as he had Gracie's signature on the contract and the surveying got underway, he would be long gone and too busy with the new ranch he intended to buy out West to worry about Gracie and her kids.

Still, he couldn't stop thinking about the crazy situation.

"What about the couple's families? Didn't the grandparents want their grandkids?"

"Nope, there was only one living relative, a grandfather on the wife's side, I think. Anyhow, he was in a nursing home and needed care himself." Wes shook his head, as if trying to make sense of it all. "Have to admit nobody expected things would come to this, especially Gracie."

Hutch took up the tale when Wes paused for another sip of coffee. "She told us she had to sign a contract of some kind right at first agreeing to be the kids' legal guardian if anything happened to the parents. It was all legal, according to their lawyer. She told us she never thought about it after that. Not until the accident."

"So, how does the ranch figure into all this? How'd she wind up here?" This was the most bizarre situation Whit had ever encountered. And he though his life was messed up.

The question made Hutch shake his head at Wes, but the younger man ignored the warning.

"A long story," Wes began slowly. "See, in the beginning the ranch belonged to Wyatt Castle, Gracie's grandfather. Wyatt bought it when land was cheap out here. After a couple of years, he married Rose. Planned on raising cattle to sell, an' he did all right at first. Their first child was a daughter. Rose named her Iris.

"Wyatt was pretty outspoken about how disappointed he was, 'cause he wanted a boy to grow up and help on the ranch. They had one eventually, but he was stillborn. Wyatt took it pretty hard. After that, he wouldn't let Iris out of his sight. Kept a tight rein on her all the while she was growing up, made her wear pants and boots like a boy. He figured he could make her into a rancher, but the tighter he pulled on that rein, the more she rebelled.

"Me and Hutch were the only help he had back then, and pretty green. Wyatt was a hard boss to work for, so we did our job and stayed out of his way. It was hard not to see what was going on in the family, though, since we took our meals with them.

"Iris didn't want to be a rancher. Rose tried to get Wyatt to loosen up, but he wouldn't have none of that. One day Iris just up and told her ma she was leavin' home. She was about seventeen or eighteen, I reckon." Wes paused, gave Whit a knowing look. "Like to broke Rose's heart."

Hutch nodded and continued the story. "Seems Iris found out she was in the family way and knew her daddy wouldn't let her keep the baby, so one night she left, just like that, without even saying goodbye to her mama.

"For a long time, nobody except Rose knew what made Iris leave, but after the baby came, she let her mama know where she was. Rose tried to keep track of her baby granddaughter, Gracie Rose, as best she could. Iris kept moving from place to place, but Rose always managed to find her. She never told ol' Wyatt she'd found Iris, though. Never told him about the baby, either. Reckon she had her reasons."

"Iris never married and never told her mama the name of Gracie's daddy," Wes added. "For a while Rose managed to send Iris a little money now and then, but after Wyatt died and left the ranch nearly bankrupt, Rose had all she could do to keep body and soul together. The old man had used all the money for liquor and gambling after the ranch started to fail.

"With the ranch operating in the red, Rose had to sell all the cattle except the bull, a cow and one heifer. She had to let the ranch hands go. Hutch and me, we offered to stay on when Rose was all but destitute. We didn't want to see her lose the ranch, so we agreed to stay in exchange for a place to stay and three squares a day. Shoot, we didn't need much money. That arrangement suited her just fine." Wes cleared his throat self-consciously and stared at his boots. "Like I said, Rose needed us."

"Why didn't Iris come home after the old man died?" Whit thought the whole story was beginning to sound like an old-time Western movie.

The pair was silent for a minute, then Hutch poked Wes with his elbow. "You tell him," he said.

Wes finished the coffee that had grown cold and set his cup on the table, pretending to find something fascinating in the bottom of the empty mug. There was sadness in his eyes when he finally looked at Whit.

"We didn't find out the whole story until right before Gracie got here last month. I mean, the attorney told us Rose had left the ranch to her granddaughter, but we didn't know any more than that. She left us a letter with her lawyer explaining the parts we didn't know."

Whit wanted to hear the rest of the story, but it was getting late. He wanted to get to the hospital before visiting hours were over.

"So the bottom line is that Gracie inherited a hard-luck ranch and the two of you, plus a couple of babies she hadn't figured on having to raise, right?"

"When you put it that way, yeah, I guess so," Hutch nodded. "But we worked plenty hard in the old days. Rose wanted us to stay on here and look after the ranch until her granddaughter came. She said we'd earned that right. Besides, Gracie needs us now as much as Rose did. She never lived on a ranch before she came here. Don't know a thing about what needs to be done."

"How does she feel about her inheritance?"

"She didn't know anything about her mother's past. Still doesn't. Me and Wes just ain't had the heart to tell her yet. Figured she had enough troubles to deal with. I mean, the past is past. So don't you go spoutin' your mouth off about what we just tol' you. She's got to deal with the future now and it ain't gonna be easy."

"Yeah, and when that new mama comes home with those two babies, she'll need us more than ever. But with you here," Wes pointed to Whit, "everything'll be easier all around."

"You know what I think?" Hutch asked, slapping a beefy hand on the table like he'd just had a light bulb moment. "I think we oughta ask Rena Blackburn to come help Gracie with the babies for a while." He turned to Whit and explained. "Rena's a widow lady in town with no family of her own. Likes helping folks out when she can." He paused, then added with a sly wink, "And she's a real good cook, too."

"She sure is," Wes said. "And I was thinking the same thing. Having one newborn to take care of is enough to keep the mama busy, but with two? Heck, ain't nobody gonna get any sleep for a long time. There's meals to cook and laundry to wash, too." He shook his head. "Too much for Gracie to handle alone, I'll wager. And Gracie's cookin' sure ain't like her grandma's."

Whit pushed his chair away from the table and stood. The men were clearly worried about the prospect of a change in living arrangements.

"I'll mention your suggestion to Gracie when I see her tonight. Right now, we've got chores to do. Oh, and by the way, I'll be sleeping in the house until I can fix a place in the bunkhouse. I'll get that done before Gracie comes home."

Hutch mumbled something under his breath and stomped out of the room"Now what the hell's wrong with him?" Whit looked to Wes for an answer.

Wes shrugged and started for the door. "Aw, he thought we'd be going to the hospital with you." He turned and shot a look at Whit over his shoulder. "So did I, but never mind. We'll see to the chores. You go on. Just tell Gracie not to worry about things here. Me 'n Hutch can manage. We always have." With that, he left to catch up with his friend. The screen door slammed behind him.

Before Whit could say anything, both men disappeared down the path toward the barn. Well, shoot. Why didn't they say something earlier? He wasn't a mind-reader. He grabbed his hat and headed out the door, fully aware of his conscience slapping him upside the head. He should have considered the old men's feelings for Gracie. Something told him he had a lot more to learn besides ranching.

"Hey, listen, I'm sorry," he shouted as he ran after the pair. "I didn't know you wanted to go with me."

The barn door slammed shut just as he reached for the rusty iron handle. Whit jerked it open and stuck his head inside. "Be ready to leave in an hour, okay?"

When nobody chunked a rock at him or told him to get lost, Whit guessed the pair had decided to cut him some slack. He had a sneaking suspicion working here would be a real eye-opener.

Back in the main house, he headed for the bathroom, stripped off his shirt and pants and filled the claw-footed tub with hot water. The only bar of soap he could find wasn't exactly manly-scented, but at least it beat his other option, laundry detergent. He sure hoped he didn't smell like a damn bouquet of roses when he showed up at the hospital. Oh well, he could always ride with the windows open.

By the time he'd scrubbed away the day's grime and donned the clean clothes he'd retrieved earlier from his truck, he found Wes and Hutch waiting in the kitchen, hair slicked back and wearing clean shirts and jeans. Their boots had even been wiped off. The pair looked like they were ready for Sunday church services.

Whit suppressed a smile. *Guess they're not so mad at me, after all.*

Chapter Five

When the three men arrived at the small hospital later that evening, the arrival of Gracie and the twins had already turned the maternity ward into a hub of excitement. Most of the nurses on the floor had never witnessed such an event. To say the babies were the center of attention was an understatement, but when Whit got off the elevator, the center of those nurses' attention quickly changed. Tight-fitting jeans and dusty boots had never looked so good.

Every nurse and aide within looking distance sighed collectively when Whit stopped at the nurses' station to ask Gracie's room number. He couldn't help overhearing their comments as he walked away.

"Wow, that's some booty," he heard one of the aides remark.

"How'd you like to go home with that one?" another asked with her hand over her heart.

"Mmmm, I hope his wife appreciates him," the head nurse said, sorting a stack of files on the desk. "That hunky cowboy is way too good to waste."

Ears burning, Whit sped up his steps.

The crusty old cowboys making their way behind Whit caused a few raised eyebrows, too, but not because their shuffling walk was sexy. They tipped their hats to the ladies, anyway.

Whit knocked gently on the half-open door of Gracie's room and stuck his head in. "Feel like having company?"

Gracie motioned him in. She was tired, but her eyes lit up when Wes and Hutch followed Whit into the room.

"Howdy, Gracie," Wes said. He approached the foot of her bed, hat in hand. "Ever'thing okay with you and the little ones?"

"We're fine, Wes." Her eyes met Whit's and her face grew warm.

Uncomfortable with the situation and their surroundings, the three men stood around the bed holding their hats and shifting from one foot to the other.

Gracie was a little embarrassed, too, remembering the intimate circumstances they'd all shared only a few hours earlier. Still, if it hadn't been for these three, she would've been all alone when the babies arrived. She shuddered at the thought of what might've happened without them.

"There's chairs over there, if you'd like to sit down," Gracie said, indicating the padded wooden chairs along the wall.

Hutch didn't hesitate to accept the invitation. Wes pulled up a chair, beside his friend, but Whit declined.

"I'll stand, if you don't mind." Behind him the door opened and a young nurse wearing yellow scrubs with teddy bears tumble-printed on the smock-like jacket bustled into the room.

"Time for vitals check," she said, placing a thermometer in Gracie's mouth. "When we're done here, you can walk down to see the babies. The doctor has finished checking them but they'll be staying in the room with you tonight, Gracie. Since they were born at home, the doctor wanted you to rest today. The nurses down there are delighted to have them a while longer." She smiled at Whit. "I'll bet the new daddy's anxious to see his little family members."

Gracie's eyes widened in panic. The thermometer in her mouth was the only thing keeping her from shouting "No! He's not their father!"

Whit backed away from the bed. He opened his mouth to correct the mistaken identity, but Wes quickly stood to give Whit a jovial slap on his back.

"Sounds good to me," Wes said. "Let's have a look at them little buckaroos, right, Hutch?"

"Sure 'nuff," Hutch agreed, staying seated.

Whit scowled.

Gracie groaned.

The nurse removed the thermometer from Gracie's mouth, smiling all the while. "It's not every day we have twins in the nursery. In fact, I don't remember the last time that happened. Bet you're mighty proud parents, aren't you?"

She patted Gracie's shoulder. "I'll help you get up so you can show off the little ones. Their bassinets are in the first row by the observing window." Then she laughed, handing Gracie a robe. "Actually, they're the only ones in there."

Gracie slanted a look at her visitors and scooted to hang her legs over the side of the bed. With the nurse's help, she donned the cotton hospital robe and cautiously stood beside the bed.

"Not too fast, now. Lean on your hubby, if you need to." The nurse put Gracie's hand in Whit's. "Now, you two go see those precious babies. Don't hurry."

Heat rose from Gracie's cheeks right up to her scalp, but she kept quiet. If the nurses wanted to think she had a husband, she'd let them, as long as Whit didn't blurt out the truth. Besides, she would be going back to the ranch in a couple of days. She'd probably never see these people again. But she didn't object when

Whit slid his arm around her waist as they slowly made their way to the nursery.

Wes and Hutch were already there, noses pressed against the window, making silly sounds and waggling their gnarly fingers at the tiny babies.

"Looky there, Wes," Hutch said with a twinkle in his eye. "I think that one smiled at me." A wide grin split his leathery face. "Is that the girl or the boy?"

Wes guffawed and pointed to the beribboned card at the front of the bassinet. "See the blue ribbon right there? Blue's for the boy, old man. The girl's got the pink one." He poked his friend in the ribs. "Never you mind, Hutch, we'll get 'em dressed proper when they come home. Then you'll be able to tell them apart."

Hutch nodded. "Yeah, that boy'll need some jeans and boots soon. The little girl, too. We'll take 'em to Shepler's. Buy some decent hats for them, stuff like that."

Looking at the tiny newborns, Gracie's heart filled with love. The twins were her family now. How awesome was that? And how scary. What if she wasn't a good mother? She knew next to nothing about babies this young. She had a lot of questions for the nurse before she took her little family home.

She'd been relieved when the doctor assured her the babies' early arrival hadn't presented any problem except for their need to be fed often for the next few weeks. They were healthy, normal babies with good weight. A pair to be proud of—and she was. Oh, she truly was.

She slid a sideways glance at Whit. Why was he frowning? He'd stepped away from the window almost as soon as they'd reached the nursery. Now he leaned against the wall across from the viewing area, one hand stuck in his pocket, the other holding his Stetson. Didn't he like babies? Not that it mattered. The babies weren't his responsibility. But he could at least pretend to like them.

Gracie sniffed indignantly. She wasn't going to let anyone spoil this moment. Not even Mr. Too-Sexy-To-Be-Safe Carter.

"Did you notice they both have dark hair?" She poked Wes's arm.

Wes nodded. "Yep, sure did. Too bad their hair ain't red like yours."

"Doesn't matter. Lots of children have different hair color than their mother. Look at me. I'm a redhead, but my mother was a brunette."

Hutch rubbed his chin. "Come to think of it, both Rose and Wyatt had dark hair, too. Wyatt had that straight Indian-black hair, but Rose's was dark brown and shiny, like sweet sorghum molasses."

A melancholy look settled over the old man's face and his voice softened when he spoke Rose Castle's name. Gracie wondered if the old cowboy had cared about her grandmother as more than just his employer?

Before she could give more thought to that probability, Wes and Hutch bombarded her with questions about the newest additions to the Castle ranch. Some of their suggestions for names were a little too bizarre and she told them so. Tex and TexAnna weren't quite what she had in mind. Neither were Roy and Dale or Blue and Bonnet. Wes explained she'd be called Bonnie for short, but Gracie still refused to agree.

"No odd or unisex names, fellas. I want them to have ordinary names that have a meaning. Don't fret. I'll decide soon."

From his vantage point behind Gracie and the men, Whit observed the goings on with guarded emotion. He preferred not to get too involved in any family-type situations. He'd just left a nasty one with his father and his younger brother, Brody, back in San Antonio. He wasn't eager to get embroiled in another. The sooner he finalized the deal with the ranch owner, the better.

Of course, he had no way of knowing what the situation was between Gracie and the two men standing beside her except for the fact that she owned a ranch in financial trouble and her geriatric ranch hands were all the help she had. The old boys were so protective of Gracie, Whit assumed they cared about her. Then again, they could simply be worried about whether or not they were going down with the failing ranch.

Whit tried to sort through the inconclusive information he'd learned from Wes and Hutch, but he couldn't concentrate for watching Gracie. Standing between burly Wes and bent-over, arthritic Hutch, she looked small and vulnerable. Not strong enough to handle the business of a large spread like the Castle ranch.

His real reason for taking her job offer pestered him like a buzzing mosquito and that left him disturbed and uneasy. Why should he care? The offer was a basic one. All he wanted was the section that followed the rim of Caliche Springs and ended at the west line fence where there was access to the main road. That would leave Gracie plenty of acreage to use however she pleased and still give LGS enough land for their exploratory geological survey.

But it wasn't fair for Gracie to agree to the lease without knowing that LGS really planned to build an exclusive community of executive homes after they convinced her to sell them the land outright. That sort of underhanded dealing is what stuck in Whit's craw.

Sure, the homes would appeal to celebrities in search of the peace and quiet found in the surrounding hill country. They'd be the kind of homes that would bring top dollar and garner the company much-needed recognition, not to mention a financial booster shot.

A community of that caliber would be successful, Whit was certain. There were enough celebrities and oil executives in Texas to make the project a smashing sell-out. And Whit would be all the wealthier for it.

Gracie's called softly through the fog of his thoughts.

"Could someone please get me a drink of water?" She turned away from the window, her face ghostly pale. Whit moved quickly, catching her in his arms just as her legs gave way. He knew then he had a tough decision to make. He couldn't walk away now. There was too much at stake.

Wes hurried off to find a nurse, but one was already zipping down the hall with a wheelchair before he had a chance to ask for help.

"Sometimes a new mother is too weak to stand for very long." The nurse secured Gracie in the chair and hurried her back to the room. "She'll be fine after she rests a bit."

Wes and Hutch followed the trio down the hall, but waited outside Gracie's room until they were given permission to see her. Both wore looks of sheer terror, even though the nurse assured them a second time that Gracie was fine.

Whit thanked the nurse after she had checked Gracie's vitals and made sure her patient was comfortable.

"I feel silly," Gracie said. "I've never fainted before in my life."

"You never had two babies all at once, either," Hutch said. "Hey, Whit, wasn't you gonna ask Gracie about something?"

For the life of him, Whit couldn't remember what Hutch was referring to. He lifted his shoulders in a shrug. "Was I?"

Hutch gave him a wilting stare. "About a housekeeper," he whispered hoarsely and elbowed the younger man in the ribs. "Remember?"

Rib-punching that hard can jumpstart the memory process pretty fast. Whit rubbed his ribs. "I do now. Gracie, these two thought it would be a good idea to ask one of the ladies in town to help out at the ranch for a few days after you and the babies come home." He turned to the men for further support. Damned if he was going to take the blame for their idea if it didn't work out. He didn't even know the Blackburn woman.

Gracie raised up on her elbows. "Absolutely not! I don't need any . . . oooh." Her face turned a sickly shade of green right before she collapsed back onto the pillows.

Whit grabbed a kidney-shaped basin from the bedside stand and shoved it under her chin. Wes and Hutch hurried out of the room, not a minute too soon.

After Whit took care of the basin, he dampened a washcloth with cool water and wiped her face. Gracie managed a half-smile of defeat. "I guess you're right. Some help at home would be nice for a while. Who did you have in mind?"

"Rena Blackburn," the older pair mumbled in unison from where they stood at a safe distance just inside the door.

"Whoever you recommend, as long as she's competent, I guess it's okay. Remember, I can't pay her much, though."

The men were clearly relieved to know their meals would still be on time and their laundry taken care of without the interruption of tiny baby schedules. They knew Rena would work for what they were prepared to offer her out of their combined savings. They'd never been big spenders.

Whit chuckled, but wasn't about to admit he thought the idea was a good one, too. He didn't look forward to having youngsters underfoot. Of course, he planned to be gone long before the twins were old enough to walk, anyway. Of course he was.

Gracie and the babies came home after five days. The old-fashioned doctor who looked after the twins in the hospital was in no hurry for her to leave. He wanted to make certain the newborns were strong and healthy—and they were. At a birth weight of six pounds for the boy and five pounds seven ounces for the girl, they were gaining enough to go home. When Gracie told the doctor she would have plenty of help he agreed to release the little ones with her.

It wasn't too many days after they arrived home before the two babies fell into a routine and Gracie was able to enjoy three or four hours uninterrupted sleep at night. During the day, she even managed to grab a nap in between feedings, sleeping when the twins did, but otherwise, she occupied her enforced recuperating time by reading baby magazines and asking the new housekeeper a million questions.

Rena Blackburn turned out to be a virtual Mary Poppins with the twins, as well as a wonderful source of information for the brand-new mom. Every day, Gracie gained a little more self-confidence in her role as a new mother. However, the same couldn't be said about how she felt as a woman.

Yesterday she caught herself staring at Whit while he helped Wes repair the front porch. He'd removed his shirt in the afternoon heat, affording Gracie a heart-stopping view of six-pack abs and snug Wranglers resting dangerously low on his hips. There just wasn't anything finer to look at than a cowboy and his jeans.

When he glanced up, their eyes locked in a heated gaze that made her heart skip a beat. She refused to believe it was anything more than the hormonal change in her body since the twins' birth. The last thing she wanted was an involvement with Whit Carter. Her life was complicated enough right now. Besides, she didn't even know if he was married.

After nearly four weeks of being tied to the house with baby feedings and learning all the things new mothers needed to know, today Gracie decided to take advantage of the napping babies and use her free time for taking a walk.

The day was sunny and hot, but a brisk breeze helped keep the temperature bearable. She was beginning to like her new home state more and more.

In the kitchen, Rena Blackburn was mixing up another of her special cakes. The aroma of her breakfast cinnamon rolls still lingered in the air.

Gracie plucked one the men had obviously missed and carried it with her to the door.

"I'll be in the barn if you need me before time to help with lunch," she told Mrs. Blackburn, before she went outside.

"You go on and don't worry your pretty head, honey. I'll call you when the little ones wake up."

Rena stopped stirring and looked up from the bowl of cake batter, one hand on her ample hip, the other waving a wooden spoon at the new mother. "You know, Gracie, I think it's time you switched the babies to a bottle. They're what. . .almost five weeks old now? Nursing those two has just about done you in. You're tired all the time and hardly ever take time to rest."

"I'm fine, Rena. Really I am," Gracie assured the woman. "But, I promise to ask the doctor about it next week when I go for my checkup."

Gracie loved having Rena at the ranch every day. The older woman insisted on spoiling Gracie and the babies. Wes and Hutch didn't lack for her attention, either. They were both head-over-heels infatuated with the widow and her cooking. Mostly her cooking, Gracie thought wryly.

"And those babies will grow just fine on formula," Rena said. "I'll pick up a few cans and some bottles on my next trip to the store." She went back to stirring the batter, smiling as if she'd just solved the world's biggest problem.

Bottles and formula were expensive, Gracie thought as she left the house, but the idea of having a little more free time sounded wonderful. Not that she didn't love cuddling Max and Susie, but the ranch's shaky finances and the worries of how to pay for the much needed repairs to the house and barn were still hanging over her head. There was very little money left in the bank from the surrogacy contract after paying for everyday ranch expenses.

Since leaving Minnesota after the accident that took the lives of Rob and Gina Renfro, Gracie had learned their home actually belonged to Rob's grandfather living in a nursing home. The sale of the property went to cover his costs. The money from the couple's life insurance policies was placed in a trust for the twins to receive when they reached twenty-one years of age.

The ranch was turning into a costly venture and Gracie wasn't about to add to her money woes by ignoring Mother Nature's way of cost-cutting. There had to be another way out of her dilemma. What she needed was some quiet time to think things through. She'd dealt with problems rougher than this nearly all her life. Well, almost as rough. She could handle this one, too. She owned a freakin' Texas ranch, for gosh sakes. All she had to do was learn how to run it. And that's where Whit came in.

Cutting across the yard, she made her way to the fenced in barnyard. The last bite of cinnamon roll left a sugary rim around her mouth. She licked it off, wiped her sticky hands on the back of her shorts and went inside the barn where Clementine and Junior were resting away from the blistering sun. And oh, that sun was hot. She couldn't decide which was worse - the hot, arid winds that often whipped through the hills, drying up everything in sight or the days when the humidity was so high you could wring water out of the air. Or the gulley-washers, as Hutch called the occasional sudden cloudbursts that seemed to come from nowhere. Who the heck invented them? Oh, and those Blue Northers that swept down from north of the Red River bringing part of Oklahoma with them to dust everything in sight? Those were definitely something Gracie could live without.

So far, she'd experienced every type of weather imaginable since she'd set foot in Texas. Even so, the rugged beauty in this big state known for its pump jacks as well as good-looking cowboys constantly surprised her. It really was "a whole other country", just like the ads boasted. And she was slowly beginning to like it. Imagine that.

Whit Carter was a whole other kind of cowboy, too. One that stirred the kind of feelings she'd rather not have. She had too many responsibilities to deal with at the moment. As always, there was no time to indulge in dreams.

She walked through the open barn door and immediately wrinkled her nose at the mixed odors of pungent manure and old hay. The distinct smell was one she doubted she'd ever get used to, no matter how long she stayed in Texas.

Two resident yellow barn cats eyed her expectantly from behind a rusty bucket, then scampered off with an indignant meow of displeasure when she walked past them empty-handed. Only Clementine's soft lowing, mingled with little Junior's satisfied sucking sound as he ate, broke the silence.

Gracie made her way to the stall where the animals stood. Clementine *moo'd* a friendly greeting as Gracie approached.

"Hello, you two." Gracie spoke softly, careful not to get too close to Junior while he was eating. The calf was growing into an energetic youngster with dangerous hooves and the ability to butt anything that got in his way. Gracie was smart enough to keep her distance. She found an empty grain bucket, upended it and sat down to wait for Junior to finish his mealtime.

Being around the cattle was a new experience for her. She'd never had a pet of her own, not even a stuffed teddy-bear. Come to think of it, she'd had quite a few new experiences since coming to Texas. Admittedly, the most disturbing was having Whit Carter around on a day to day basis. He made her think about things she knew she couldn't have. She'd been a lot safer back in Minnesota when all she had was her dreams.

Dwelling on her past was something Gracie seldom allowed herself to do. In fact, most of the time she avoided it, but once in a while the painful memories crept in. Like now.

The hollow feeling in her chest wasn't new. She'd experienced the same emptiness many times, especially during her teen years when her mother's real illness became more and more evident. Oh sure, waiting tables at the diner provided enough income to pay the rent on the little apartment she and her mother shared. Riding the bus every day had saved the cost of a car, too. Even so, money was tight and there'd been little left over for extras.

By the time Gracie was fifteen, she'd become adept at hiding money from her alcoholic mother. She dealt with Iris's angry tirades and sorrowful apologies. Worry was Gracie's constant companion for as long as she could remember.

When it finally became necessary to place her mother in a rehab facility, Gracie had just turned twenty-three. Her meager bank account didn't last long after that, so she began looking for ways to pay the mountain of medical bills that accumulated during the year of her mother's treatment.

The answer to her financial woes came a week after Iris Castle died. Gracie knew right away she'd made the right choice. Surrogacy would provide the money she needed to pay off the debts and she'd be helping someone in the process. Nine months out of her life and then she could begin a new one. What could go wrong?

Looking back now, she was shocked at how naïve she had been. Just when she thought she would no longer have to be responsible for anyone but herself, life had thrown her another curve, making her sole guardian of the twins before they were even born. What had God been thinking? No, what had *she* been thinking when she signed those agreement papers?

Junior made a snuffling calf sound when he finished eating and moved from away from his mother, shoving his wet nose against Gracie's shoulder. When she didn't respond immediately, he pushed harder, like a child eager for attention.

Gracie laughed at the calf's insistence, grateful to leave her dismal thoughts behind.

"Hey there, sweetie, you're looking handsome this afternoon." She stroked the calf's soft face.

"Why, thank you, ma'am."

"What—?" Gracie jumped up at the sound of the deep, male voice, sending the bucket flying across the barn floor.

Whit stood in the doorway, a shaft of sunlight accenting those sexy, faded jeans and his equally sexy grin, which by the way, wasn't faded at all. Suddenly, heat engulfed her entire body. Her face burned, along with other less obvious parts of her anatomy. Her reaction embarrassed her.

"Darn you, Whit, you shouldn't sneak up like that." She bent to retrieve the bucket, taking the opportunity to regain her composure. She hated that his presence could send her into total idiocy without warning. How juvenile for her to feel this way. *Behave, Gracie. You're a mom now, for goodness sakes.*

Whit took the bucket from her shaky hands. "I'll put that away for you." His grin widened.

If he hadn't been standing so close, Gracie might have been able to think more clearly. Might have even told him to take a hike. But no, she just stood there enjoying the way his eyes crinkled when he smiled and the way his denim shirt hugged his broad chest. She refused to look any lower. Not that she hadn't wanted to, but that was dangerous territory she didn't intend to explore.

"What are you doing out here?" Gracie kept her gaze directed at his face, but found it equally distracting to look at his mouth. She stared anyway.

He tipped his hat back, giving her a clear view of his dark, delicious eyes. "I was going to ask you the same question. Didn't I hear you call the barn a smelly old place the other night at supper?"

Gracie couldn't decide which was more dangerous, his mouth or his eyes. Concentration was a challenge. "I might have. You have to admit the fragrance in here isn't from a rose garden." A smile tugged at the corners of her mouth, in spite of her effort to appear nonchalant. "To be truthful, I was checking on Junior while Max and Susie napped. I haven't had much opportunity to get outdoors lately. The babies still eat every four hours." She checked her watch and sighed. "And they're due to wake up soon."

"That so?" Whit moved closer, his gaze roaming her face. "Then, how about letting Mrs. Blackburn feed them this afternoon so you can take a break and ride into town with me. I need to get some supplies from the co-op. Wes and Hutch are pounding nails in the fence behind the barn, otherwise I'd send them."

A pleasant shiver danced along Gracie's spine. Whit's invitation was oh, so tempting. But it wasn't the idea of spending a couple of hours alone in his company that warmed Gracie's cheeks. A too familiar heaviness filled her breasts.

She looked down and immediately wanted to die. Two damp spots blossomed across the front of her shirt. Could she be more humiliated?

"She can't. Feed them, I mean."

Embarrassment tied her tongue in a knot. Her face felt on fire. Oh, dear lord.

Whit had the good manners to blush beet-red when he realized what she meant. "Oh, yeah, I forgot," he mumbled and averted his gaze.

Oh sure, he's staring the other way now. Why on earth did this have to happen in front of him? She'd never be able to look him in the face again.

"I . . . have to leave." She dashed out of the barn and didn't stop until she reached the house. By that time, the entire front of her shirt was wet.

Whit let her go. Actually, he stood silently and watched her fly down the path. What else could he do without embarrassing them both? How stupid not to remember she was nursing her babies. Showed how much he knew about mothers and babies. Worse yet, the rush of heat coursing through his blood made him feel like a fool. He had no business acknowledging his attraction to Gracie. No business at all. His business here was simply to finalize the sale. A transaction he hadn't discussed with Gracie yet. Delaying was only making matters worse, but for the life of him, he couldn't explain what was holding him back.

The calf nuzzled his wet nose against Whit, leaving a string of calf slobber on the leg of his jeans. Absently, he ran his hand down the calf's nose, giving it a pat. "Guess I'll go to town alone, huh, Junior?"

He'd parked his truck behind the bunkhouse earlier, so he headed off in that direction. The image of Gracie and the reason for her sudden departure had stirred up some uncomfortably intense sensations below his belt buckle and not for the first time, either. He needed a cold shower and a change of clothes before he headed into town.

Lately, the more he was around Gracie, the more his focus on the project slipped. How the hell was he supposed to convince her to trust him when he didn't even trust himself

Just then the first bars of *The Eyes of Texas* blared from his cell phone. With an impatient scan, he read the caller ID and swore. Baby brother was on his case again.

Chapter Six

"I'm telling you, Whit, if you don't get that woman to sign that lease pretty damn soon, I'll come out there and close the deal myself. We need to get that project underway. Time is money, remember? And that ranch is right in the middle of the acreage we're after. You're supposed to wrap up everything by the end of this month. Today's the fifteenth and you haven't even made an offer. What's your problem with the Castle woman? I thought you told Dad she'd be a pushover."

Yeah, that was when he thought the ranch owner was an elderly widow with money problems. Whit ground his teeth at his younger brother's tirade. Anyone would think Brody was the company president already, the way he carried on.

"I know what day this is, little brother. And I know what I told Dad. Don't get your boxers in a bunch. I'm handling this last one my way, remember?"

He needed Brody poking around the ranch like he needed a poke in his eye with a sharp stick. Gracie would ask too many questions and Whit didn't have the right answers yet.

"I need more time. You just stay in Texas City and keep crunching numbers. I'll handle this deal my way."

"Sounds like you're dragging your boot heels on this one, big brother." A long pause, then, "Okay, I'll give you two more weeks, but you'd better have something in writing by then."

Whit started to remind his smart-mouthed sibling that nothing at LGS was his to give yet, but Brody cut him off with a rude directive and disconnected the call.

It was no secret the youngest Lovett had always wanted control of LGS. Whit admitted that of the two brothers, Brody was better qualified to run the company because he actually liked working in the family business. It wasn't Whit's fault he was born first. Wasn't his fault, either, that he preferred a much simpler way of life over the mega-privileged lifestyle his parents enjoyed. Hell, if he had a choice, he wouldn't even be a Lovett.

The bunkhouse was empty when Whit entered. He was glad Wes and Hutch were still out repairing the broken fence. A few minutes of privacy was a much welcomed change from his usual day.

He headed for the recently renovated two rooms with a view he occupied in the back of the bunkhouse and stretched out on his cot with his arms crossed above his head. He let his thoughts settle around the dilemma that felt like a prickly pear cactus stuck in his conscience. He needed more time alone to examine this whole situation with Gracie and her ranch land.

Acquiring the acreage needed for the family business was the reason Whit was here in the Hill Country in the first place. He hadn't wanted to take on the project. It wasn't honest. In fact, he'd argued about that very point with his father and Brody right before he left Texas City and again when they met in San Antonio to go over some incomplete contracts. Whit wanted to leave the company immediately. His father had vehemently argued against it. Brody couldn't wait for Whit to disappear. Three men with three different concepts of success. Three different solutions for achieving it.

Whit figured the whole problem was caused by having too much money in the first place. The Lovett name was well known in Houston area society, thanks to the shrewd business acumen of Whit's grandfather. Leasing land at minimal cost for geological surveys had paid off handsomely. Dabbling in real estate and the development of some of the first exclusive gated communities in the area had boosted the financial status of the Lovett family to almost indecent proportions. Whit's father, W.C.L. Jr., inherited the massive trust when the senior Lovett died. He continued to amass the family fortune, driven by the need to have it all. That all-consuming drive left little time for his family.

Whit's mother was always involved in several auspicious fund-raisers for charity every year. Of course, Whit didn't even try to keep up with her whereabouts any more. He'd given up on that about the time he turned twelve.

That summer, right after his birthday in May, he'd been lucky enough to be shipped off to his maternal grandparents ranch in Kerrville. At least there he'd known he was loved, even if he was a skinny city boy with more brains than brawn. Spending time with Gram and Pop at their ranch was the only good thing in his life back then. He didn't even notice the absence of his mother's visits at first. He was thirteen when he finally figured out she was actually ashamed of her parents and that made Whit ashamed of the entire Lovett clan.

His maternal grandparents lived simply, with little formal education and even less material riches, but they gave Whit a fortune in love and understanding. His love of ranching and horses was deeply imbedded in his soul by the end of that first summer with them. By the end of the next summer, his body had filled out, honed by the demands of hard, physical work at his grandfather's side. Gram's wonderful home cooking hadn't hurt, either.

Ah, sweet memories. Whit smiled. Pop had given him his first riding lesson on a docile mare named Lulu. By the time summer ended and he returned to school, he had graduated to riding Major, Pop's own black gelding. When Pop and Gram took him to his first rodeo in San Antonio to celebrate his thirteenth birthday the next summer, Whit thought he'd flat out die of happiness. That was when he decided ranching was what he wanted to do for the rest of his life.

His father's reaction to Whit's career choice had been anything but supportive. No son of Whitman Lovett. Jr. was going to become a common cowboy. Whit spent the next two years at a stuffy East coast prep school. When he came back to Texas City, his homecoming surprise had been a new baby brother. He was sixteen years old and had absolutely no interest in a diaper-clad sibling.

With money to burn and little discipline, Whit's high-school years were rebellious, to say the least. When his father's approval seemed unattainable no matter what he did, Whit decided to take a different approach. In college, he learned all he could about land acquisition, development and marketing. He had a natural talent for making profitable deals and after a time, built a reputation as shrewd as his father's. He should've been happy.

Life was privileged and the Lovett name gave him access to everything he needed and pretty much all the luxuries he could ever want, but didn't need, including a high-maintenance wife named Cecily, one of Houston's wealthiest socialites. It took him two years to discover his mistake. That was three years ago.

Since then, he'd been regarded as the black sheep of the family. His mother blamed him for the divorce. Whit never corrected her. It was easier than explaining the truth.

Now, his only interest was ranching. As soon as he finished this final project for his father, he intended to buy his own ranch, and if the notion struck him, he might even buy two. He had plenty of money, and pretty soon he'd have the time. After all, he wasn't even forty yet. He had lots of years ahead to do whatever he damn pleased.

He was glad he'd used a different name when he'd first met Gracie. He had a feeling the two old ranch hands were suspicious of him. They never questioned him, but Whit caught them watching him on several occasions when they thought he was unaware of their scrutiny.

Gracie was another matter altogether. Whit hadn't quite figured her out. She'd been less than talkative in matters concerning her past. Of course, he couldn't censure her for that. He'd been pretty close-mouthed about his own past.

The fact that he'd seen her so intimately when she'd gone into labor, then again when he'd turned into Mr. Midwife and delivered her twins, not to mention watching her take care of her little ones at home, stirred something deep inside his gut. A yearning he'd almost forgotten. But he remembered, with a rush of clarity, how to push away that ache around his heart. And that's exactly what he did. Much safer that way.

Whit sat up and shoved off the bed. What sentimental rot he'd been thinking. So she was a good-looker and he felt some old-fashioned lust when he was around her. He wasn't about to get tangled up in a relationship that included kids. No way. Kids were for people who could raise them right, be good role-models, take them to ball games and stuff. He was the last man on earth for that job. Being parents should be a lifetime endeavor, not a short-term course that included only weekends and holidays.

Gracie intrigued him, though, even tempted him to try for a temporary romantic interlude, but Whit knew he'd be shot in both knees if he tried that sort of thing. Her bunkhouse bodyguards would be all over him like ugly on an ape. And besides, Gracie deserved someone a little less jaded than him, someone who could promise her "forever". His track record would never take any prizes and his "forever" plans didn't include any women. No, he'd be better off finishing up here, then leaving the Castle ranch for good. There were lots of places in Texas where he could buy that ranch he dreamed of. Maybe nothing as beautiful as the vistas and valleys of the Hill Country, but he'd find some place suitable. Maybe Montana. There'd be other women, other places, other times.

Showered and sporting clean jeans and shirt, Whit grabbed his hat and strode out of the bunkhouse. His boots crunched on the gravel path as he made his way to the main house. Wes and Hutch would probably be headed that way soon, so he decided to join them for a cup of coffee and a piece of Rena's super-delicious Texas Sheath Cake before he went to town. The tantalizing aroma of the dark fudge cake topped with pecan-loaded icing had teased his palate when he passed the kitchen earlier, reminding him of the delicious home cooking he'd enjoyed in Gram's kitchen.

The screen door squeaked when he opened it and he mentally added WD-40 to his list of things to purchase when he went to town. He was halfway to the kitchen table when the soft sound of a baby's whimper caught his attention. But it was the faint words of a lullaby that froze him right where he stood. How the hell had he missed seeing her?

There she sat in the rocker by the window, singing softly while she nursed one of the twins, totally unaware of Whit or the world around her until he groaned.

When Gracie looked up with that angel smile of hers, Whit nearly lost his way in the depth of her sea-green eyes and the lushness of her lips. Only one kiss, he thought. What could it hurt? He took a step toward her.

The only thing that saved him from doing the unthinkable was the baby's lusty cry at being interrupted. Whit did a warp-speed three-sixty and shot out the door with a giant leap off the porch. He was all the way to the barn door before he remembered his cake. Well, hell.

Embarrassment stung her cheeks for the second time that day as Gracie watched Whit tear out of the house like a bunch of fire ants had climbed up his pant legs. She'd thought he had already left for town.

"So much for thinking we had the house to ourselves, huh, Max? Guess we'd better stick to the bedroom for mealtimes from now on."

She tickled the baby's tummy. Max whimpered, then squirmed and filled his diaper.

"Well, thanks for that very explicit answer, little man. Your manners need a lot of work." Humming softly, she headed down the hall.

On the way to the bedroom to change Max's diaper, Gracie heard boot-stomping in the kitchen again. Had Whit returned? Her heart *gallumped,* even though she braced herself against the silly sensation. She hoped it was Wes or Hutch. She wasn't ready to face Whit right now.

Max squalled louder as she cleaned him up, obviously not liking the situation any more than Gracie did. His wails woke

Susie and the tiny sweetheart let her mama know she wasn't happy about having her nap interrupted. Another diaper change, a pacifier for Susie until Gracie could feed her, a clean outfit for Max, and so it went. From then on, there was no time to indulge in daydreams. The twins were all Gracie could handle at one time. Dreams had to wait.

Rena had taken a cake out of the oven before she left for a dental appointment. Good thing, too, because the boot stomping had come from Wes and Hutch, not Whit. Gracie caught the two helping themselves to cake and coffee and making a first-class disaster of the kitchen. If Rena had seen them messing up her freshly-scrubbed kitchen, the pair would've certainly suffered her wrath. As it was, they hee-hawed their good luck at having free rein with the cake.

"Enjoying yourselves?" Gracie transferred Susie to Wes while she put Max in the playpen.

Wes stopped eating long enough to cradle Susie in his arms, making silly, *goo-goo* sounds at her. His actions were so out-of-character, Gracie had to stifle a laugh. She didn't want to interrupt the bonding of the old man and the baby.

Hutch watched silently. The forlorn look in his eyes almost broke Gracie's heart. She knew the older man was afraid to hold the babies because of the tremors that had become noticeably more pronounced lately.

"If you want to hold him on your lap, I'm sure you won't have a problem, Hutch," Gracie said. "Want to try?"

Hutch shook his head. "Nope, I'll wait until he's walking. Then the two of us can go fishing. I'll show him where his great-granddaddy and I used to catch those big ol' catfish."

Gracie took Susie from Wes and laid her next to Max, then helped the men with their coffee and cake. She cleaned up crumbs and wiped up spilled sugar, all the while trying not to show her excitement at the mention of her grandfather. She might as well have tried to hide an elephant in the middle of the room. The chance to learn more about Wyatt Castle was the very thing she'd been waiting for.

She hurriedly poured coffee for herself and crossed her fingers that Susie would wait a little longer for her feeding.

"You fished with my granddaddy, Hutch?"

Hutch nodded. He saucered some coffee, blew on it and sipped. "Sure did," he said after he'd taken another sip. "Right down on the banks of the Blanco River." He shoved a bite of chocolate cake in his mouth. "Mmm-mmm, that Rena sure can cook. I hope she bakes one of these every week, right, Wes?"

Wes had his mouth full, too, but his head bobbed up and down in agreement. Neither one of the men was in a hurry to end the tasty coffee break.

Susie wasn't interested in anything except her next feeding and her high-pitched wail let everyone know it. Gracie huffed out an exasperated sigh and retrieved the fussy baby from the playpen. "You two might as well look after Max while you finish stuffing yourselves, okay? I'm going to feed Susie. She's the only one around here who hasn't eaten lately." She disappeared into her bedroom.

The men weren't about to be rushed. Gracie knew she wouldn't get any information out of them until after they'd polished off at least half of Rena's chocolate cake. One of these days, she was going to give the pair the third degree about Wyatt Castle and this ranch. The only way to learn how to be a ranch owner was to start at the beginning.

While Susie nursed, Gracie rocked and tried to keep her thoughts from bouncing around, but the mental list of questions for Wes and Hutch just wouldn't go away. The disturbing image of one particular cowboy kept popping up uninvited, too, about as welcome as a Texas dust storm. This was so not what she wanted in her life right now. Or was it?

Until now, her life had been so focused on her mother's care and trying to stretch her meager salary, there'd been little time for a personal life. True, there'd been one "almost" relationship with one of the regulars at the diner, but it had taken only two dates for Gracie to realize she was only one of many in the truck driver's travels. Besides, leaving her mom even for one evening, had brought near disastrous consequences. After finding Iris at the neighborhood bar, roaring drunk and hitting on every man in the place, Gracie resigned herself to a single life as her mother's caregiver. Her dream of a place to belong would always be just that, a dream.

Gracie found Wes and Hutch on the front porch with little Max when she came looking for them. Susie, the smaller of the twins and the one who slept the most, dozed peacefully in her mother's arms. Max was wide-awake and enjoying the attention from the men. The late afternoon sun hid behind a bank of clouds that cast cooling shadows over the yard, providing shade for the few hens determined not to move to their newly-refurbished coop. Chickens had a mind of their own, Gracie recently discovered. She wished she had nerve enough to land one of the pesky roosters in a frying pan.

"Hi, guys." She sat down next to Hutch.

Wes held Max on his knees, totally infatuated with the boy. With any luck, Gracie hoped she could resume the previous conversation with the men. She yearned to hear all about her Texas relatives. To think her unknown past had included ranching and cowboys and everything she'd held close to her heart in her dreams was almost more than she could comprehend.

The only thing her dreams hadn't held was the "mommy" situation she found herself in now. But when she looked at Max and Susie, she couldn't imagine life without them. The problems facing her might seem monumental, but Gracie wasn't a quitter. Security was one thing her children deserved and she'd provide it, no matter what she had to do. And that included becoming a rancher.

"Everything okay, Wes?" She smiled at the old cowboy and her son.

"Yup. This boy's bright as a new nickel. He's gonna make a fine cowboy, you wait and see." He bounced Max lightly in his arms.

Gracie laughed. "He's not even six weeks old yet, Wes. I think it will be a few years before he'll be herding cows."

"Me and Wes ain't getting any younger, missy," Hutch spoke up. "We aim to start our little buckaroo doing some cowboying soon as he can sit a saddle." Hutch planted his hands on his knees and pushed up from his chair. "Now, I'm gonna finish a little whittlin' project I started. I'll be back around supper time." He left the porch, his shuffling walk clearly an effort for his arthritic limbs.

Well, darn, Gracie thought. Hutch was the one she'd hoped would give her some answers about the history of the Castle family. She was beginning to think there was a plot to keep her from digging into her ancestors' past. Oh, well. She shifted the sleeping Susie in her arms and turned to Wes, who was serenading an uninterested Max with a gravel-voiced version of *San Antonio Rose.*

"Wes, when did the first Castle come to this area? Did it always belong to Wyatt and Rose? Where did they live before they came here?" She knew she was asking too many questions, but if she didn't, she was afraid she'd never find out the truth about her background. So she persisted.

The old cowboy stopped singing. His bushy brows knit together in a thoughtful frown. "Now, that's a lot of questions all in one breath, missy. Don't know that there's time enough now to get to all of 'em, but I can tell you this."

Max squirmed then and Wes hoisted the child up on his shoulder, his big, gnarled hands holding the baby secure and safe as if he'd done it hundreds of times. "There's a big book somewhere in Rose's bedroom that she always wrote in every night before she went to bed. You might find some of the answers you're looking for in that, if you can find where she kept it." He stood and began gently rocking side to side until the fussy babe quieted. "I'll put him in his crib now. Poor little tyke, he's plumb tuckered out."

"You're evading my questions," Gracie said, following Wes into the bedroom. "Why is it you and Hutch turn silent as stones when I ask about my grandparents? Is there some dark family scandal hanging over the ranch? Or a resident ghost?"

Wes laid the sleeping Max in his tiny bassinet, then turned to Gracie. "Like I said, find Rose's journal and you'll likely get your answers. Most of 'em, anyway. It ain't for me to say." Quietly, he left the room.

Gracie put Susie in her own little bassinet and crossed her fingers in hopes the two would sleep for another hour. Then she made her way down the hall into the bedroom where Rose Castle had spent the last days of her life. If the journal was anywhere in this lavender-scented room, Gracie vowed to find it. She needed to know where she came from . . . and where she belonged.

She found several boxes in the closet, some stuffed with faded remnants of dress fabric and spools of thread, others held multi-colored skeins of yarn, knitting needles and several unfinished pieces, but so far, no journal was among the mementos.

Thinking Wes had returned when she heard someone enter the room, Gracie didn't look up from where she sat cross-legged on the floor sorting through a box of papers.

"Are you sure Rose kept her journal in here?"

The papers she'd just finished sorting through were mostly bills of sales and invoices—ranch business that Gracie supposed she'd need to study later. For now, though, she put them back in the cardboard box and turned to see why Wes hadn't answered her.

"Oh, you're not Wes." A tiny spark of excitement sizzled through her body.

Whit leaned one shoulder against the door frame, his arms crossed lazily against his chest, Stetson pushed back on his head to reveal those dark, sultry eyes. A low chuckle rumbled from his chest. "Last time I checked, I wasn't." He took a step inside the room. "Disappointed?"

She wasn't about to answer that, thank you very much. But she might admit, only to herself, of course, that Whit affected her in ways that were dangerously exciting. "Uh, no, I thought Wes had come back." She started to get up, but when Whit knelt beside her, she changed her mind and stayed where she was.

"So, are you looking for something specific or sorting stuff to donate to the local charity?"

"Actually, I was just sorting through these boxes because I wanted to make more room in the closet for other things." The fib slipped off her tongue so easily, Gracie felt a bit of shame. Still, she didn't want to reveal the real reason for her search just yet. "Is there something you wanted? I thought you'd gone in to town for supplies."

"I'm on my way now. Just wondered if there was anything special you needed."

Kneeling next to her, his face was only a whisper away from hers. Gracie felt that whisper when he spoke and her heart shot straight into hip-hop rhythm. What she needed was for Whit Carter to take his sexy self out of reach, because she suddenly had the darndest urge to plant a hot, wet kiss right on his tempting mouth. And the images following that particular urge would likely keep her awake again tonight. This had to stop!

"Uh, no, thanks, nothing." She licked her lips, swallowed back a sigh and scooted over to put a bit more distance between them.

Whit didn't seem to notice. In fact, he closed the gap easily when he took both her hands, lifted her to her feet as he rose and turned her to face him.

"Gracie. . ."

"Hmmm?" Oh, lord, she couldn't take her eyes off his mouth. Why was she so obsessed with his mouth? Hello! Because you want him to kiss you, dummy. She leaned toward him without realizing it until he spoke and his breath feathered across her face.

"I thought I'd get that paint you wanted for the porch. You said white, didn't you?"

Gracie came down from the clouds with a bump, nearly falling face first into his chest. "Oh. Paint. Uh, yes, white will be fine." Her face was now in a permanent state of burning embarrassment. Had she really believed he could be interested in her?

She pulled her hands from his, stumbling back awkwardly over one of the boxes. *Clumsy is good. That'll impress him.* Why that was important, she didn't have a clue right now. It just was.

"So there's nothing else you need from town?" He'd hurried to catch her when she stumbled and still held her lightly around the waist. "Nothing for the twins, either?"

"No. Thanks, anyway. I don't need a thing." *Liar, liar, pants on fire.* What she needed wasn't found on a shopping list. In spite of the warning from her sensible inner voice, Gracie didn't move away, just stood there absorbing the heat from his warms hands. When he dropped them, she immediately felt deprived. How pathetic was that?

Whit stood close enough for Gracie to see something almost wicked flare in the way he looked at her. Their intense gazes locked for only an instant, but it was long enough to ignite a blaze of desire within her entire nervous system.

"I'll see you later, then," he said in that slow, seductive Texas drawl that never failed to weaken her knees.

Gracie watched, her whole body still tingling, still wanting, until Whit disappeared from her view.

What would've happened if she'd followed her urge to kiss him senseless? The shameless temptation stayed with her the rest of the day.

Chapter Seven

Whit sped down the road toward Peabody, cursing himself six ways to Sunday. He was a fool to ignore the signals he'd sensed Gracie was sending back there. The electricity generated between them was enough to light up all of South Texas. And she'd felt so damn good when he'd had his hands around her waist. He should've just kissed the living daylights out of her and gotten it out of his system. He was pretty sure she would have kissed him back. Yeah, that's what he should've done, all right.

But then, that would have put a crimp in his plans to obtain the lease and he didn't want to screw that up. Once he finalized this deal, he'd be out of the company so quick, he'd make a Texas dust devil look like it was standing still.

This project went against all his business ethics, even though he'd agreed to it before he knew the property belonged to Gracie. LGS didn't need to buy this particular land to stay in business. If anyone needed them, Gracie did.

He'd heard rumors in town about the finances of the Castle Ranch and Wes had pretty much validated them the other day when they were in the barn. It didn't take a genius to see the rundown condition of the buildings or the lack of stock and feed supplies. The ranch was on a fast train to failure. Whit wasn't about to be the conductor who took it to the station.

Brody had been pretty certain of the survey location and he was rarely wrong in his calculations. Whit respected his brother's expertise in that area, even though he disagreed with some of his other business practices. Brody was a carbon copy of their father. Another reason the younger Lovett would be better as next in line for company prez, instead of Whit. Whit had never fit the mold of a company executive. Never wanted to. He wore his cowboy boots with jeans, not with custom-made Western suits. He actually liked getting his hands dirty, a habit his ex-wife had deplored.

The last time Whit had driven over some of the Castle ranch property, he'd gotten some pretty crazy "what if" ideas in his head. There were ten sections lying unused, part pasture, part cactus-covered range. Mesquite brush and rocky ground made up the rest of it. Gracie's sole cattle herd consisted of Hercules, Clementine and Junior, plus one other recently purchased heifer due to freshen in another few weeks. Not exactly a money-making herd.

Whit hadn't been able to check out the entire range, but if what he'd seen was any indication, the ranch wasn't as hopeless as he'd first thought. Possibilities had been popping up in his head on a regular basis the past week. They didn't include selling any land to LGS, either.

He was so engrossed in his thoughts, he drove right past the feed store and had to circle back around the block. Good thing there weren't too many locals on the street to take notice. He pulled his truck next to the loading dock, went in and took care of business. Forty-five minutes later, he was loading his purchases in the back of the truck when a much too-familiar voice called his name. Damn. He slammed the tailgate shut and walked around the truck.

"What the hell are you doing here, Brody? I still have two more weeks, remember?" The sight of his younger brother grinning at him from behind the steering wheel of a sleek, black Jag tied a knot in Whit's gut so tight it hurt, but he refused to let it show. He propped one booted foot on the pickup's narrow running board, rested an arm on the hefty side mirror, and willed himself to stay calm.

"Nice set of wheels, little brother. New?" The extravagant vehicle was obviously a recent purchase. Brody bought new cars like other men bought power tools. Always black and always expensive. Image was important to Brody Lovett.

Brody took a slow inventory of his older sibling's dusty jeans and scuffed boots before he flicked an imaginary speck of dirt from his own custom-tailored shirt. "Yeah, big brother, this is the kind of luxury you get when you run with the big dogs. Too bad you've decided to trade your college degree for a ranch hand's garb. That outfit you're wearing must be right out of TV-land, huh? I'll bet you even do that funky boot-scooting stuff on Saturday nights, too. Are you working your macho magic on the reluctant Ms. Castle?"

Whit held his tongue, but it wasn't easy. Brody liked nothing better than to get under his older brother's skin. This time, it wasn't going to work.

"I don't need magic to get my job done." Whit shoved his hat back and returned Brody's stare with one of his own. "You want to tell me why you're here?"

"Buy me a steak and I'll tell you all you want to know."

"You buy the steak and I'll listen," Whit countered. He was anxious to hear what Brody was up to, but he damn well wasn't buying the steaks. Not this time.

Brody's laugh sounded more like a derisive snort. "Short on cash, are you? Okay, where's a good place in this one-horse town to get a decent meal?"

"Follow me, little brother, just follow me." Whit climbed into his Silverado and sped toward Wimberley with his jaws locked and his temper on the rise. By the time he reached the local steak house just outside the town he'd had enough time to make a decision on the first stage of his plan.

Deliberately choosing to park his truck on the far side of the restaurant, Whit waited impatiently for Brody to join him. As Whit knew he would, Brody parked his Jag on the far side to avoid contact with the dust-covered, hard-working pickups occupying the spaces nearest the door. Whit had a nasty urge to key his little brother's precious status symbol as they walked across the lot.

When the two walked through the door of The Lucky Longhorn, Brody took one look around and let out a sarcastic "Yee-haw!" Whit ground his teeth and clenched his fists to keep from rearranging his sibling's face.

"Watch yourself," Whit warned quietly. "That smart-ass attitude will get you in a heap of trouble here, if you're not careful. These ranchers don't take kindly to anyone bad-mouthing their lifestyle."

Brody shrugged. "Does that include you, Whit? Are you a cowboy now?" Condescending sarcasm dripped from his words as sharp and acid as a slice of lime in an ice cold Corona.

"Don't worry about what I am. Just keep your mouth shut and quit acting like the snob you are." Whit slid into a booth at the back of the room and motioned for his brother to do the same. "And no smart remarks when the waitress comes, either."

Surprisingly, Brody acted the proper gentleman when he ordered his steak rare after Whit ordered the smoked brisket special. He even asked for a beer instead of his usual expensive Scotch when Whit ordered a Lone Star.

That put Whit on the defensive. Little brother had something up his sleeve. Something that spelled *trouble* sure as Texas had George Strait.

"Okay, let's have it. Why'd you show up here when I told you I had things under control?" Whit lifted the longneck to his mouth, drank deep and waited for Brody to answer. A premonition that he wasn't going to like anything his brother had to say settled in his gut like a lump of cold beans.

Gracie took the beef and noodle casserole Rena had left for their supper out of the oven and set it on the table next to a bowl of fresh salad. The fragrant loaf of bread the older woman baked earlier was sliced and ready to be slathered with butter. Ice cubes tinkled in tall glasses when Gracie poured the tea over them.

"Eat up," she told the men. "I think Rena has plans to go visit her sister in Goliad soon. These wonderful meals of hers won't be around much longer."

Wes and Hutch sat on opposite sides of the kitchen table, eagerly anticipating their supper. They admitted to Gracie not long ago that their own cooking left a lot to be desired in the months after Rose's death. Fried bacon and beans from a can get mighty boring, Hutch had told her. Now, the two men couldn't say enough good things about the meals coming their way.

"I'll bet you won't let us starve, though. You oughta ask Rena to give you a few pointers." Hutch looked sheepish, then said, "Not that your cooking ain't good, you understand."

"Especially when you're hungry, right?" Gracie punched Hutch's shoulder lightly, then took her seat.

"You better stop while you're ahead, old man." Wes grinned at his friend's blunder. "By the way, I wonder what happened to the boy?" For reasons only he knew, lately Wes had taken to calling Whit *the boy*.

Whit's willingness to tackle the many tasks needed around the ranch pleased Gracie, but for some reason the two older men were still less than happy with his presence. Oh, they liked the extra help, but Gracie could tell they didn't entirely trust Whit, even though he was saving them a tremendous amount of work.

She wasn't quite sure what they based their suspicions on, but she really didn't care. Whit was the best thing that had happened to the ranch since she'd arrived. He had seen to the repairs right from the first, making the leaky roof number one on the list. That alone made him worth his salary in Gracie's eyes.

As far as she was concerned, he was simply a cowboy hired to help out on the ranch. Just because he happened to be good to look at didn't make him a slacker where work was concerned. The fact that he caused too darned many restless nights filled with dreams she shouldn't be having . . . well, that was something Gracie definitely needed to deal with. There would be disastrous consequences soon, if she didn't.

"You day-dreamin' again, missy?" Hutch chuckled and helped himself to the casserole. He passed the dish to Wes and winked.

Gracie felt her face grow warm. She reached for her glass of iced tea, sipped and took her time answering. She wasn't going to admit she'd been wondering about Whit, too.

"I was thinking that the front porch needs scrubbing before Whit starts to paint it. He's getting the paint when he gets the other supplies in town. And another thing," she turned to Hutch, "can't you keep those wretched chickens in their pen? The house looks worse than the chicken coop. Besides, it's not healthy for the twins to have all those feathers flying around. Bad enough the house doesn't have air-conditioning or ceiling fans. This awful heat makes Max terribly fussy."

"I'll see what I can do. You just make sure the little ones are fed and happy. Me and Wes'll see to the rest."

"What about Whit? Don't you think he'll be working, too?" Gracie looked from one man to the other.

Wes shrugged and Hutch shook his head. It was clear as glass that neither one of them wanted to talk about the absent cowboy.

"Well?" Gracie prompted.

Wes buttered a slice of bread. "I figure Whit will be wantin' to get things fixed up fast so he can hit the road. That's what I think. The other day he drove clear to the south forty in his pickup. Said he was checking fences, but hell, those fences don't even need to be there. There's nothing in that section but mesquite trees and scrub brush. Be good for goats, if we had some, but Hercules and the cows, they don't like it out there."

"That's right," Hutch said around a mouthful of salad. "Maybe it'd be a good idea to sell off that part of the land, Gracie. You could run the cattle on the west pasture and get by just fine. I told your grandma a long time ago she oughta' sell some of them acres back when prices were good, but she was too stubborn to let any go. Instead, she darn near went bankrupt trying to keep her head above water. Didn't make sense to me then and it don't make sense now."

"Why do you suppose she wanted to keep all the land?" Gracie finished her salad and pushed back her plate. She wanted to keep the conversation going, so she passed the casserole around again. The men usually left right after their evening meal and she didn't want to let that happen just yet.

"I 'spect she planned all along on leavin' the ranch to you. She wanted it to be worth something when she died. Rose Castle was a stubborn woman, but as good-hearted as they come. That's why she gave me and Wes a place right here on the ranch to live out our days. She knew we had no place else to go."

"I still think Whit's got something up his sleeve," Wes said. "There are times when you'd swear he had money in his pocket, but then again, some days he doesn't have a lick of sense when it comes to cattle. He asked me why there weren't any horses on the ranch, too. Said he planned to buy some of his own someday. Don't sound like he means to stay if he's thinking like that. And if he's got money to buy horses, what's keeping him around here?"

What was keeping him around here? Gracie took her dishes to the sink, rinsed them off and thought about what Wes had said.

"Well, at least, he fixed the leaky roof and repaired the porch rails. He said he'd paint the porch next. And," she paused, thinking of all the things Whit had done in the short time he'd been there, "he told me he was working on an idea to help get the ranch out of the red. That should count for something." And maybe it meant he didn't intend to leave so soon.

She cleared the rest of the table without asking the men if they were finished eating or not. The sinking sensation whirling in the pit of her stomach at the mention of Whit leaving the ranch for good was worse than the morning sickness she'd had with the twins. Better not to even think about it.

If she hurried, she could get a load of laundry done before the twins woke up hungry and fussy, as usual. She couldn't remember the last time she'd gone to bed before midnight, but it must have been before she ever set foot in Texas.

"How about some cake?" Hutch brought the leftover chocolate cake to the table.

"Coffee would go good with it," Wes said and rose to get the cups, motioning for Gracie to sit down.

Gracie smiled at their attempt at domesticity. The two had become a little more helpful in the kitchen when Rena wasn't there. Probably wouldn't last long, though.

"Got enough left for me?" Whit sauntered in, hung his hat on the wall rack and eased his lanky body into a chair at the table.

Gracie spun around from where she stood at the kitchen sink. With the crazy way her heart somersaulted, she knew better than to attempt to speak, so she just nodded and set a clean plate and cup in front of Whit. Hopefully, her insides would settle down before she embarrassed herself.

"Thought maybe you were gone for the night," Hutch said, helping himself to a chunk of cake.

Wes poured coffee all around without saying a word. Gracie pushed a bite of cake around on her plate with a fork, waiting for Whit's explanation and trying not to seem too interested.

Whit took his time answering the question implied in Hutch's statement. Last time he checked, he was over twenty-one and capable of taking care of himself. He wasn't aware of any curfew rule when he's signed on as ranch manager, either. Hell, he made sure every damn chore on Gracie's TBD list was finished before he fell into his bunk at night.

Every morning at breakfast, she handed him another list of to-be-done stuff. So far, he was right on schedule, as far as repairs were concerned. Luckily, she hadn't questioned him about the extra supplies or the lumber for repairs that he brought in. Neither had the bunkhouse boys, but Whit suspected they knew what was happening. Gracie assumed he'd added the items to their account at the feed mill and he hadn't corrected her.

Some evenings, he burned the midnight oil trying to figure out the best way to turn Gracie's ranch into a lucrative operation again. Other nights it was the ranch owner herself who kept him awake until dawn. Those nights were the ones that tested his self-control, especially when the clear view of Gracie's bedroom window afforded him an occasional glimpse of her enchanting shadow moving across the room in a wash of silvery moonlight. Nights when the heat generated by images of Gracie in bed with him caused him to break out in a cold sweat and embarrassingly turned him into an adolescent with wet sheets.

Heat stung his face when he turned off his fantasies and realized there were three inquisitive pairs of eyes watching him. Had he groaned out loud? Aw, hell.

"I, uh, ate at the Lucky Longhorn tonight after I picked up the supplies. Had a hankering for smoked brisket and a cold longneck." He picked up his fork and attacked the cake, avoiding the curious gazes. "Only had one beer, though."

"Brisket, huh?" Wes raised an eyebrow. "I heard tell the Longhorn's got some of the best." A wistful sigh escaped his lips. "Me and Hutch don't eat out."

Curiosity got the best of Gracie. "What in the world is brisket?"

"It's a cut of beef that's the test of a good Texas cook. Takes a lot of experience to smoke a brisket just right," Wes explained, a hint of Texas superiority underlying his words.

"Really? I'll bet I can cook one just as good as the Longhorn's chef." Gracie challenged. "Show me the recipe."

All three men guffawed. "Ain't no chef at places like the Longhorn, just a cook. No recipe, either." Hutch told her. "Just good ol' Texas know-how."

"And you need a smoker, too," Wes added. "Used to have a dandy one around here a long time ago. Never used it much after Wyatt died. Don't know what happened to it. Rose must have tossed it in the scrap pile."

"Never mind," Whit said, giving Gracie a smile way too close to patronizing to suit her. "It's a Texas thing. You don't need to worry about learning to cook a brisket. You've got your hands full taking care of your little buckaroos."

"You three think you're so superior, just because you were born in Texas." Tears stung her eyes as she spun on her heels and marched the last of the dishes over to the sink. "I'll have you know I can learn to do anything around here that needs doing. You'll see."

With that, she flounced out of the kitchen, leaving dirty dishes in the sink and the men staring, dumbfounded, after her.

"What in tarnation put a bee in her bonnet?" Wes wondered aloud.

"I'm pretty sure it was that remark about the brisket," Hutch said. "Gracie's kind of touchy about being a greenhorn around the ranch. She's been trying hard to learn, but let's face it, there's certain things just come naturally to a native Texan. I don't think she'll ever learn to cook black-eyed peas and cornbread on a wood stove like her grandma, but she does all right on the gas range. And Rena's been giving her some tips, too. You have to give the girl credit. She didn't know sic'em from c'mere when she first got here. Now, at least she knows the difference between a cow and a heifer. And, by the way," Hutch shot Whit a stern look, "you ought to let her know when you're not planning to be here for supper. Just good manners." He finished his cake, drained his coffee mug and stacked his dishes before taking them to the sink.

Wes did the same, then followed Hutch out the back door. "Tomorrow's Saturday," he reminded Whit. "Breakfast's at seven."

Whit sat alone at the table wondering what the hell had just happened. One minute he was enjoying chocolate cake, the next he was being first-degree'd by the men. Gracie had basically given him the cold shoulder when he first came in. Dammit, what did he have to do to get on the good side of these people? He shoved away from the table, ready to head for his bunk, when the sink full of dirty dishes caught his eye. Impulsively, he rolled up his sleeves and got to work.

Gracie stood quietly in the doorway, studying the scene at her kitchen sink. Whit washed each dish and utensil carefully, rinsing them before placing them in the plastic drainer. He was so absorbed in his task, Gracie knew he hadn't heard her approach.

Just as well, she thought. She liked looking at him, especially when he was unaware of her scrutiny. He wasn't extremely tall, maybe just under six feet, but every inch of his toned body was packed with sex-appeal. She'd seen her share of average, good-looking men when she worked at the diner, but there was something different about Whit. Something she couldn't quite define. Something that excited her from the first moment he came flying over the fence to rescue her and caused her body to respond in ways she never knew existed.

Yeah, she was totally fascinated by this cowboy. She hoped he planned to stick around for a while. There was more to Whit than just his sexy appearance, though. A quality she'd never seen in any of the men she'd encountered in the past. He exuded a strength and self-confidence that tempted Gracie to depend on him way too often. That wasn't a good thing. It was only a matter of time before he hit the road. He'd already told her he had other business to take care of soon.

She prided herself on her own self-sufficiency and never, ever intended to be dependent on anyone. She'd seen dependency at its worse in her mother and vowed a long time ago she would never allow that to happen to her. She couldn't afford to let that happen with Whit. And yet she couldn't help wondering what the result would be if she did.

Whit bent to retrieve a dropped fork and almost lost his balance when he caught sight of Gracie watching him from the doorway.

"Hey, Gracie," he said, tossing her a smile guaranteed to light her fires.

She couldn't resist smiling back. The sight of him doing dishes as if it was a normal occurrence sent warm images of home and family flashing through her mind.

"Kitchen duty isn't part of your job, you know." She moved toward him, her heart doing roller-coaster dips at breakneck speed. "I should have cleaned up the dishes earlier."

"No problem. I'm almost finished here. Not sure where all the stuff belongs, but I reckon you'll find things eventually." He turned back to his task and drained the water from the sink.

"Thanks." Gracie hoped he couldn't hear the pounding of her runaway heart. She didn't know why, but she suddenly felt the need to explain her actions earlier. "Sorry if I acted snippy earlier. It's just that sometimes Wes and Hutch make me feel so inadequate because I'm not a native Texan. I know they don't mean to, but . . . ."

Whit's arm found its way around her shoulder. "Hey, don't let those two get you riled. They're just jealous because they've never been outside the state of Texas." He gave her shoulder a squeeze. "It's a nice night. What say we go sit on the porch and you can tell me all about life North of the Mason-Dixon line."

Gracie took her time contemplating Whit's suggestion. With the twins down for the night, his invitation was too tempting to pass up. Oh, what the heck? She let him lead her down the hall and out the front door. His arm slipped from her shoulder to circle her waist. The warmth of his touch excited her, yet at the same time the anticipation of what might happen held her heart captive. In that heady moment, the sensation of free-falling into space made her head spin. And she liked the feeling. She really did.

The night was sultry sweet, a soft breeze brushed gently against her face. They sat side by side on the porch steps. It seemed like the natural thing to do when the slight pressure of Whit's arm encouraged Gracie to rest her head against his shoulder.

"So," he said, "tell me all about sweet Gracie Castle."

Chapter Eight

If Whit had spoken gibberish Gracie wouldn't have cared because all she heard was his sexy, unmistakably Texas drawl when he called her "sweet Gracie".

What was it about sitting beside him in the moonlight that fueled her imagination? Did she really want a cowboy of her own?

The realization that she wanted Whit in every way possible wasn't exactly a surprise. She just hated admitting it. He'd appeared in her dreams every night since his arrival, no matter how hard she tried to chase him away. But in her dreams there'd been no plans for a future together, only the moment of passion in Whit's arms. She was realistic enough to understand that Whit was just a cowboy passing through. Still, it couldn't hurt to stay right where she was for a little while longer.

"Earth to Gracie." Whit cupped her chin in his hand and turned her face toward his. "Hey, are you there?"

The intensity of his dark gaze captured her, held her frozen in his embrace. She was close enough to see the question burning in the depths of his velvet-brown eyes—an undeniable spark of desire that matched her own. Her breathing accelerated, her pulse skittered crazily. The spark ignited a red-hot flame when Whit leaned closer and touched his lips to hers.

Oh, yeah, she was there all right. If a body could burn from the inside out, Gracie's was sizzling right this minute. Never had she imagined a simple kiss could cause such an erotic flood of heat deep enough to touch her very core. Heat that stroked her like a lover's touch, full of temptations and the anticipation of unknown delights.

Suddenly, Gracie didn't want *simple* anymore. She turned into Whit's embrace and kissed him back like she'd done so many times in her dreams—hot, wet and wild. Reality was *sooo* much better than dreams.

She pressed closer against the hard wall of Whit's chest, feeling the thump of his heartbeat on her breast. The flood of heat that began when his lips touched hers now swirled through every part of her body. When her need grew almost unbearable, she pulled him closer, molding her curves to his angles. She whispered his name into their kiss, breathing his breath, tasting his taste.

Her senses reeled with new awareness. Every inch of her body tingled. If a single kiss could excite her to the point of losing all rationality, did she dare imagine what being loved thoroughly by this man would be like?

He honestly meant to keep the kiss simple, but after the initial shock of her ardent response, Whit realized nothing about Gracie would ever be simple. His feelings for her weren't simple, either, and that bothered him, but not enough to stop kissing her. Not enough, at all.

Angling his head to gain better access to her sweetness, he slid his tongue between her soft lips, silently cheering when she let him in. His hands caressed her back, her shoulders, her neck, then cradled her head as he deepened the kiss with an unspoken question.

Their kisses escalated, suggested, promised. She melted against him, her body fitted intimately against his. There was little doubt in his mind Gracie knew where this would lead in a very short time. Knowing she'd been the one to initiate the level of intensity made his pulse race at break-neck speed and his jeans become much too tight, much too soon. Lord have mercy, he wanted her right here, right now. And that would never do.

With the taste of her still lingering on his tongue and his smoldering need ready to burst into flames, Whit reluctantly, painfully, moved away from their embrace. There was nothing he wanted more than to continue this lovemaking right into her bedroom, but he wouldn't. Neither would he make her feel foolish for her enthusiastic responses. After all, he'd wanted them as much as she had. Much more, if he was honest.

So instead of giving in to the moment, Whit gently lifted her hands to his lips and brushed a kiss across each fingertip.

"I'm sorry, Gracie. I was way out of line." He searched her face for understanding. Hoped to see it reflected in her eyes, instead of hurt or embarrassment. The last thing he wanted was to cause her to feel uneasy around him.

Well, surprise, surprise. Evidently, his concern was unwanted. Gracie's green eyes glittered and Whit swore he glimpsed shards of gold in their depths. The combination was electrifying.

"Don't you dare apologize, Whit Carter," Gracie said through clenched teeth, her voice barely above a whisper. "Don't you dare." She jerked her hands away and got up to leave.

"But, Gracie, I only meant . . . " Whit stood, tried to recapture her hands, but she wouldn't let him.

Green fire flashed in her eyes. "No! If you apologize, that means you're sorry you kissed me. And you didn't kiss me. I kissed you. My choice, do you hear? And I won't apologize for it. I'm responsible for my own actions and that's that."

Chin out and spine rigid, she hurried back inside. The screen door squeaked on its rusty hinges right before it slammed shut behind her.

Whit waited a few bewildered minutes before heading for the bunkhouse and his lonely bed. He sat on the side of his bunk, toed off his boots and kicked them across the room. What the hell had just happened back there? One thing he knew for certain, there'd be no sleep for him tonight.

A sudden impulse had him scrabbling for his boots. He yanked them back on and headed for the door, careful to keep his actions quiet. He damn sure didn't want to wake the old fellows.

Outside, he breathed in the cool, night air hoping it would clear his mind. Thinking always came easier when he walked, but even if it was possible for him to walk around the entire Castle Ranch tonight, there wouldn't be enough time to resolve how he felt about Gracie and the twins. Scared didn't begin to describe the way his nerves jangled and his mind spun out-of-control.

With his hands jammed in his pockets, he started off down the path toward the west pasture. Maybe if he walked far enough he'd figure it out. Hell, how *did* he feel? He had to start thinking about it sometime. Might as well do it now.

Two hours later, Whit slipped quietly back into his bunk, no further along in his thinking than he'd been when he left. This time, he was careful not to flip his boots across the room. He'd never be able to explain his nocturnal stroll to Wes and Hutch.

Gracie tiptoed into her bedroom, undressed quickly and pulled on her faded night gown. She checked the sleeping babies, made certain they were dry, then stroked their heads ever so softly before sinking into the security of her own bed.

The night was inky dark. No stars broke through the blackness, only a few low clouds hiding the waning moon. The room held shadows from the night light she'd left on, but they were soft shadows. Not like the scary ones she remembered from her childhood. Turning over on her side, she pulled the sheet up from the foot of the bed and tucked it under one arm. Even though the night was warm, Gracie never went to sleep without the security of a light cover, a habit she had yet to overcome.

Events of the day came flooding back as her eyes drifted shut. Was Whit lying awake, too? She doubted that. He was probably sleeping as soundly as the twins were, the few minutes of hot and heavy kisses they'd shared already forgotten.

She punched her pillow. Men! And he had the audacity to apologize. That really ticked her off. Did he think she'd never been kissed? She wasn't naïve. She knew what she was doing when she kissed him. And she'd been more than ready for whatever might follow. *So there, Mr. Whit Carter. You lose. Apology not accepted.* With that, she flopped over and willed herself to sleep.

"Sunday's supposed to be a day of rest," Gracie murmured sleepily the next morning as she gathered a sobbing Susie in her arms and padded barefoot into the kitchen to warm a bottle. Thank goodness, the twins had adapted to formula without too much trouble. They were almost two months old now and growing stronger each day.

Max was beginning to interact a little, while Susie was happy just to snuggle in Gracie's arms. Both babies were easy to spoil and Gracie was careful not to hover over them too much.

The uneasiness she'd felt when her life had been turned upside down by the birth of Max and Susie was slowly disappearing. Her daily routine had definitely changed, but for the better. She had a home here at the ranch. Security for her, as well as the babies. That was something she'd never had.

So what, if she didn't know every little thing about ranching or motherhood. She'd gotten used to the animals, even if she still didn't like the chickens. She loved her precious babies more than she'd ever thought possible. And she was trying her darndest to become as much like a Texan as possible without filing for citizenship. Honestly! Texas pride was certainly alive and well at the Castle ranch. So was the testosterone level. Thank goodness Rena was around for female support.

Gracie took the warm bottle of formula out of the pan of hot water, shook it and tested it on her forearm. Whit had surprised her a few days ago by installing a microwave, but she wasn't comfortable using it to heat the babies' bottles.

She settled down in one of the rockers on the front porch. The air was warm, but she kept the baby wrapped in a soft summer blanket, hugging her close. Susie ate eagerly and noisily while Gracie's eyes were drawn toward the bunkhouse.

At this early hour, the three men were probably still asleep. Chores were done on schedule six days a week, but on Sunday it was agreed that everyone could sleep a little longer. Usually, the older men pursued their personal pastimes the rest of the day. Hutch liked to whittle when his arthritic hands let him. He'd proudly shown Gracie the collection of carved horses and riders he'd created through the years. Now the figures were prominently displayed on a tier of shelves next to his bunk. Wes spent his free time perusing ranching magazines. Gracie suspected they brought back memories of better times when the Castle ranch had prospered. Sometimes, Whit took off in his truck for a ride around the ranch.

She'd almost asked to go with him the last time, but then she remembered the babies. Times like that caused old resentment to rear its ugly head, but Gracie forced herself to push it away. Whit had better things to do than get involved with a single mom. Especially one with twins to raise. Max and Susie were her responsibility, just like her mother had been. And Gracie was well acquainted with making changes in her life to accommodate someone else's needs. Hadn't it always been that way? A smidgen of bitterness still remained in her heart, but she was working on getting rid of it. Not the easiest thing she'd ever done.

Susie finished her bottle and promptly fell asleep in Gracie's arms, but Gracie lingered, reluctant to leave the peacefulness of the early morning and the soothing motion of the porch rocker.

As she coaxed a burp from Susie, her mind wandered from her own hidden heart's desires to the painful realization that life wasn't about her dreams anymore, but about finding a way to care for the family she'd acquired by accident. She needed a permanent home for the three of them. And Wes and Hutch, of course. The two men would always be a part of her life from now on. The Castle Ranch was the perfect place for all of them. All she had do was perform a miracle and find a way to make it profitable.

Since there weren't any miracles scheduled for today, Gracie went inside to put Susie in her bassinet and start breakfast. Sunday was Rena's day off, so today's meals were left up to Gracie. She hadn't yet decided what to cook for the noon meal. She couldn't begin to compete with Rena's experience in the kitchen— wouldn't even try. Maybe she'd look through her grandmother's recipes and find a real Texas dish to fix. Or maybe she should just forget cooking at all and tell the men they were on their own for meals today. Yeah, she could do that.

She filled the coffee pot with water, measured out the coffee and flipped the switch. She'd make their coffee, that was all.

Hurrying down the hall, she looked in on the sleeping babies and figured she had about five minutes to shower and dress.

Whit finished dressing and left the bunkhouse with the intention of taking an early morning drive to inspect the west section of the ranch. He'd been here for two months now and so far, he'd managed to put off approaching Gracie about leasing her land to his father's company for a geological exploration. The whole idea still didn't set well with him.

Any other time, the deal would've been finalized and Whit would have been on his way within a couple of weeks, tops, but he was still here after two months. Why couldn't he manage to put the offer on the table for Gracie? What the hell was wrong with him lately? His chance to leave LGS for good was right here in front of him.

All he had to do is convince Gracie to sign the papers. She needed money to keep the ranch running, so he was pretty sure she'd take the deal, especially when he was prepared to offer her enough for that and still make money for LGS. So where was the exhilaration that usually accompanied his deal-making skills? He was damn good at what he did, but he was having a hell of a time enjoying it now.

Rena's old Ford sedan rumbled up the road just as Whit got in his truck. Without waiting for his good sense to kick in, he swung the truck in behind her and followed her up the drive.

"'Morning, Rena," Whit said as he climbed out of the truck. "Didn't expect to see you out here today."

Rena Blackburn got out of her car, handed him two loaded grocery sacks and motioned with her head for him to follow her into the house. Before she headed for the kitchen door, she pulled an oblong covered pan from the back seat.

Whit sniffed the air like a hunting dog. "I smell cake."

"Of course, you do," Rena said, matter-of-factly. "I decided to fix y'all a nice Sunday dinner today. Where's Gracie? She take those babies for a walk already?"

Whit managed to pull the screen door open with one finger, then stuck his booted foot around to hold it while Rena went in ahead of him. "Don't think so, but I just got here myself." The scent of freshly-brewed coffee met them at the door. "She must be up and around somewhere, 'cause the coffee's made."

Rena set the cake on the table, then took the bags from Whit's hands. "Thanks. Now get yourself some of that coffee and pour me a cup, too, while I get busy fixing breakfast."

Whit did as he was told. You didn't argue with Rena, he'd learned. Not if you were hungry. He set her coffee on the counter, knowing she would drink it as she worked, and took his own to the chair by the window to wait for Gracie to make an appearance. He had just drained his cup when she walked into the kitchen, freshly-showered and looking way too delectable for her own good. Just the sight of her set his pulse racing.

Her gaze tracked from Rena to Whit and stayed there caught by his incredible smile, though she addressed her words to the older woman. "What's going on? Rena, what are you doing here? You're supposed to have the day off."

Rena shrugged. "Well, for goodness sakes, what am I supposed to do at home all by myself? Besides, I had a hankering for fried chicken today and couldn't see any sense in cooking only two pieces. Might's well cook the whole chicken while I have the pan hot. In fact, I've got two fryers, so there'll be plenty for everyone." She leaned against the counter and sipped her coffee. "Thought maybe the menfolk would like some fried okra and butter beans, too. I made another Texas Sheath Cake, too, but I'm going to rustle up an old-fashioned banana pudding right after breakfast, just in case Wes and Hutch are extra hungry." She glanced toward the back door. "By the way, where are those two old coots, anyway? Thought they'd be here as soon as they heard me drive in."

"I'm sure they'll be here in a minute," Gracie assured the woman. "Wes likes his coffee as soon as he gets up." The words had barely left her mouth when the men strode through the door, both of them grinning ear to ear when they spied the cake on the table.

Hutch nudged Wes's arm. "Looks like this Sunday's gonna be all about good eatin', huh, Wes?" They both grabbed a cup and filled them. "Is somebody having a birthday?"

Rena laughed and gave Wes a friendly rib poke as she walked past. "No, just a lonesome old woman needing company, so you'll have to put up with me and my cooking today. That a problem for you?"

Wes and Hutch shook their heads. "No problem, dear lady," Wes replied, polite as could be. "No problem at all."

Whit rose from his chair and ambled over to where Gracie had taken a seat at the table. "Well, if it's all the same to you, Gracie, I thought I'd ride out to the west section after breakfast. Want to come along?"

Acceptance was right on the tip of Gracie's tongue, but she didn't trust herself to be alone with Whit again, not after yesterday. "I'd better stay here and look after the twins. They'll be hungry again soon."

"That's not a problem. I can feed them, you know, now that they're on formula." Rena told her. "Wes can help me, if I need him." She winked at the wide-eyed old cowboy. "Can't you?"

Wes looked like he'd swallowed a mouth full of bad milk. He struggled with a half-hearted smile. "Uh, sure, Rena, if you say so."

Rena nodded, satisfaction lighting her round face. "Well, I say so."

"That's settled, then," Whit declared. "Now, how about some breakfast?"

An hour later, the truck bumped along the two-track under a bright morning sun hanging high in a cloudless, blue sky. Exhilaration hit Gracie like a double jolt of caffeine. With Whit behind the wheel and the pure joy of the moment coupled with anticipation of seeing more of the ranch land, her heart was lighter than she'd ever thought possible. She wanted to hang on to the euphoric feeling as long as possible.

She wasn't certain, but maybe the reason for her happiness was because the twins were thriving, making her days and nights easier. Or it could be because the ranch was running smoother since Whit arrived. Not making money, mind you, but keeping a roof over their heads. Wes and Hutch didn't argue as often now that Rena had agreed to stay on as cook, either. They were all settling into a routine that felt a lot like family to Gracie. Hope and security were becoming more than a dream.

She could name a hundred little reasons for the light-hearted way she felt today, but only one stood out above all the rest, Whit's bone-melting kiss.

Whit Carter might be only a temporary blip on the radar screen of her life, but after a long night of mental anguish, Gracie reached a decision. No matter how brief their time together might be, she would accept whatever Whit had to give with no regrets, knowing it might be her only chance for happiness. Knowing her heart would break when it ended.

Chapter Nine

Whit turned the truck off the two-track and guided it across the bumpy, mesquite-dotted pasture until they came to a grassy area alongside a winding creek that gurgled past a stand of live oak trees.

Gracie poked her head out the window and gave a little cry of delight. "Oh, how beautiful. I didn't know this was here." She turned to Whit. "Why didn't somebody tell me about this place?"

Her enthusiasm for something as simple as a creek in a cow pasture gave Whit yet another glimpse of Gracie's very private side. "Don't know," he said. "Maybe Wes and Hutch forgot about it. They probably haven't been this far from the bunkhouse in a long time. Want to get out and take a walk?"

"Oh, yes. Look at all the wildflowers." Masses of colorful blooms adorned the ground near the stream like a brilliant patchwork quilt.

Whit rounded the front of the truck to help her out. With her hand in his, he led her closer to the water. "Watch out for those," he pointed toward the random cactus scattered across the field. "Prickly pears are deceiving. The blossoms look pretty, but the thorns are wicked."

"How can something so pretty be dangerous?"

"How, indeed?" Whit said, suddenly somber.

Gracie pulled her hand from his, puzzled. "Is something wrong, Whit? You sound so serious. Did I insult the cactus or something? Is that another pride of Texas thing I need to learn?"

Her words drew a smile from Whit. "No, Gracie, there's nothing wrong with what you said." He recaptured her hand. "I'm sorry. Guess my mind wandered a bit remembering something else that was pretty as well as dangerous."

"Another flower?"

This time Whit chuckled. "No, definitely not a flower. A person. But the day's too nice to spoil on that unpleasant topic, okay? Let's just enjoy

"You're lucky if you've never had to pull a cactus thorn out of your hand. Trust me, Gracie, you don't want to find out. Come on, there's a shady spot a little ways from here where we can sit and enjoy the scenery."

Watching Whit spread a blanket for them to sit on, Gracie realized her breathlessness came from more than the short walk over the uneven ground. The man just plain took her breath away.

"Might as well get comfortable." He pointed toward the blanket. "This will be better than sitting on the hard ground."

She sat hugging her knees and let the quiet beauty of the countryside begin its magic. When Whit eased his lanky frame onto the blanket beside her and braced his arm behind her for support, she thought her day couldn't get much better. *Well, there was one more thing.*

Instinctively, she leaned against him, reveling in the sense of security that came with the solidness of his strength. She relaxed, confident that this was exactly where she wanted to be, if only for a little while.

"I'm still waiting to hear about Minneapolis." Whit nudged her with his shoulder.

"There's not much to tell, really. I'd rather talk about something else. Tell me about Texas," she said. "There's so much I need to learn, I don't know where to begin."

Her gaze drifted across the stream to the other side where more rocky ground rolled toward the distant hills. She smiled, "You know, I thought Texas was just flat prairies with lots of cowboys roping cattle and riding in rodeos. I had no idea there were hills and valleys like these."

"That's what a lot of people who've never been here think. It's always a surprise when they learn Texas has hills, valleys, the Piney Woods out East, the Gulf Coast beaches, as well as flat plains and dust in the Panhandle," he explained. "Rivers, lakes. You name it, we've got it. And every spot in the state has its own brand of charm."

"That sounds a lot like a tourism commercial," she teased. "It really is a whole other country, like the ad says." Gracie turned her head so she could look at Whit, surprised to find his gaze fastened on her face. How was she supposed to think when he looked at her like that?

"Yeah, sure is." His rough whisper feathered across her face as he brushed her cheek with the back of his knuckles.

His eyes darkened, intensified. Gracie was pretty sure his attention wasn't on the geography of his home state at that particular moment.

Her heart tumbled when he turned her into his chest. "Yeah," she whispered back, trying to get a better look at his mouth and keep her balance at the same time. His lips were curved in a sensuous invitation, close enough to make her shiver when he smiled down at her, yet he made no move to kiss her.

Impatient, and not quite understanding what crazy urge came over her, Gracie made an impulsive and shockingly bold decision where Whit Carter was concerned. She took matters into her own hands, literally. In one quick motion, she pulled his head down and kissed him—hard.

The next thing she knew, she was stretched out beside him, wrapped in his arms and, Glory Hallelujah! he was kissing her back and she was loving every minute.

Whit's world rocked on its axis at Gracie's impulsive move, but oh, how quickly he fell into the moment. With his mouth on hers, he explored the softness of her lips, and when she parted them, his tongue slipped in to savor the sweetness there. He felt her heart race wildly when he pulled her closer into his embrace.

Nothing could have surprised him more than Gracie's eagerness to participate. Her reluctance to end the kiss told Whit there was no mistaking where this was leading. He wasn't sure whether to be wary or very, very thankful.

"Gracie," he whispered, his words skimming across the delicate curve of her neck, "uh, sweetheart, this would be a good time to make sure you know what you're doing. Is this what you really want?"

Gracie's "yes" came out on a sigh as she snuggled deeper into Whit's arms and something exploded inside his head. He hadn't expected that answer. For a mind-blowing minute, he lost all reasoning.

"Yes," she whispered again and slid her hand inside the waistband of his jeans. Whit swallowed a groan and argued with his conscience about the right and wrong of what he was about to do.

"God, Gracie, you're killing me here."

With slow, sensuous kisses, his lips traveled from her mouth to the soft curve of her throat. When he lifted the hem of her shirt and touched her bare skin, the shock of its silkiness left him breathless. Her breasts, heavy and tempting inside her simple cotton bra, pushed insistently against his hand, an invitation he couldn't resist.

He rolled her on top of his eager body and quickly undid the restraining bra, granting him access to her bounty. Slowly, tenderly, he paid homage to each breast with his mouth, his hands.

And while he was busy there, Gracie paid her own kind of homage to him as she found him, stroked him and damn near had him firing off a rocket way too soon. He grabbed her hand, held it still when reality slapped him upside the head. What the hell was he doing? Any involvement with Gracie now would only complicate matters when he was ready to make the deal for the land lease. He didn't want to screw that up or he'd never get a chance to make his life his own.

He eased away, searching her face for a sign of understanding. But there was no understanding in those wide, green eyes, only hurt. Whit felt like pond scum for starting something he knew was wrong. Did she think all he wanted was a quick tumble in the grass? Didn't she know he would give her the pleasure of slow, sweet loving in a heartbeat if he could? But, hell, how could she know when he'd done such a good job of hiding how she made him feel. Not the easiest thing to do, either, when all he could think about was taking her to bed.

"Whit?" The puzzled look on Gracie's face couldn't have hurt more if she'd punched him in the gut.

He rolled to his side, studied her and wondered if he'd just lost the chance for something special. Something he'd thought about weeks ago but had been too focused on his own issues to admit.

"Gracie," he said, shaken but determined to put things right. "I wasn't looking for . . . I'm sorry. I didn't plan for this to happen, honestly." He was surprised at how easy that lie slipped from his lips. He damn sure wasn't sorry for anything except having to stop.

Scooting back so she could sit up, Gracie yanked down her shirt over her open bra and shot him a fiery, green stare. "So you don't want to make love with me, is that what you're saying?"

The heat in her gaze sizzled like a branding iron straight from the fire. Whit rubbed a hand over his face, surprised not to find his cheek singed, after all. "That's not what I said, Gracie. Believe me when I say making love with you has been on my mind for a long time."

"Then why . . . ?"

He sat up, took her chin in his hand and tipped her face toward his. "Because I can't give you what you need—a commitment that includes a future together." He thumbed away the tear sliding silently down her cheek. The heaviness in his chest was guilt, pure and simple.

"How do you know what I need, what I want?"

Gracie's voice cracked, became a whisper. "You don't know me at all."

He leaned closer, his words brushing against her lips. "And that's the problem, sweet Gracie. You don't know me, either."

Then he kissed her like there was no tomorrow and damned the consequences when she clung to him and kissed him back.

Gracie's hand slid under his waistband again, tugged at his zipper. This time he didn't stop her. Didn't even try. They were two adults who wanted the same thing and he was damned if he knew why, but he wasn't going to argue this time.

In an instant, his jeans and boxers were nowhere near where they should have been. But there was one more matter to take care of. He reached in the pocket of his jeans.

"Gracie," Whit whispered as he moved over her a minute later, all precautions taken care of. "I won't force you, but damn, I can't last like this much longer."

Gracie pulled his head down and put her lips to his ear. "Then do something about it, Whit, before I explode, you hear me?"

She didn't need to ask twice. Whit ground his teeth to keep from burying himself deep inside her and driving her over the edge before she was ready.

Time stood still for Gracie as Whit claimed her mouth with such tenderness, such care, she feared she would shatter into a million pieces with happiness. Overwhelmed by unexpected emotions, she pressed against his hard body, curve to angle, heartbeat to heartbeat. Nothing mattered except his touch and the way his hands reverently brailed her body while his mouth, both demanding and gentle, played havoc with her senses. Caught in an upward spiral of sensual ecstasy, she matched the urgent tempo of his strokes, taking him deeper inside where the passion she'd saved for so long waited for sweet release.

Just when she thought she could wait no longer, he whispered, "Let it happen, sweetheart. Let go and come with me."

Then the world as she knew it soared rapidly to unexplored realms before colliding with the sun. The last thing she heard before the total eclipse consumed her soul was Whit's hoarse cry as he followed her.

Something sharp was poking him in the back like a cattle prod. Whit opened his eyes slowly and tried to decide where the hell he was. The blasted sun was searing his eyeballs and something was pressing on his chest. When he realized the weight was Gracie's arm, he remembered. Oh, yeah, he remembered it all.

He'd collapsed from exhaustion, and no wonder. He'd just experienced the best sex he'd ever had. Gracie's total abandonment of her inhibitions had surprised and delighted him. What's more, her determination to please him had been nothing short of amazing. Not that he was complaining, but there was more to what he'd felt than just sex. With Gracie, he'd felt a completion, a sort of "coming home" satisfaction that scared the hell out of him. Commitment wasn't in his plans. Not now, not ever again.

Careful not to awaken Gracie, he rolled off the blanket and got up. Puling on his jeans, he walked to the water's edge. He ran his fingers through his hair and splashed his face with the cold water. How the hell was he going to tell Gracie the real reason he'd come to the Castle Ranch? How was he going to explain leaving her after what they'd just shared?

This place wasn't even close to where he planned to settle down. He wasn't even sure he wanted to remain in Texas. There was plenty of land in Colorado or Montana he could purchase. All he wanted was a ranch of his own, one he created from the ground up. A place far away from the Lovett family and all its greed.

He wanted horses and cattle roaming wide open fields as far as you could see, not noisy cities jammed with skyscrapers and covered in smog. He wanted to be his own boss, make his own mistakes. He'd been waiting a long time to get to this place in his life, too long to let this chance slip out of his hands. But what the heck was he going to do about Gracie? About his new and unexplored feelings for her?

He didn't hear her approach, didn't know she was right behind him until she wrapped her arms around his waist and rested her head against his back.

"I can't believe we've been gone all morning," she said. "I should get back to the house. Rena will wonder what's happened to us." She moved around to his side and gave him an intimate smile that messed with the doubts in his mind. "I hope we'll come here again."

When she looked up, he saw trust and expectation shining in her eyes. He couldn't think of anything to say, so he just walked away. This was the best and worst day of his life.

The low whirr of the AC was the only sound inside the truck unless you counted Whit's nervous finger-tapping against the steering wheel. He hadn't even turned on the radio like he normally would have done. Instead, he remained deep in thought on the entire drive back to the ranch house, wondering if Gracie's silence meant she was regretting their lovemaking or if she was waiting for him to say those words that were forever stuck in his throat. Either way, from now on he'd be responsible for whatever direction their relationship took. He wasn't sure he wanted that load on his shoulders but he had to tell her the truth.

He slid a sideways glance at Gracie sitting quietly beside him. She hadn't said a word since they'd gotten in the truck. He couldn't figure it out. If only she'd say something, anything to give him a clue what his next move should be. The silence was killing him. So was the knowledge that he already wanted her again.

"We're here." He stopped the truck at the house, got out and hurried around to open the passenger door for Gracie. "I'll let you out then get back to work. Tell Rena I won't be in for her Sunday dinner, but ask her to save me some chicken."

"There's no reason for you to miss the meal," Gracie told him, suddenly stiff and way too polite. "What's so important that it can't wait until later?"

Uh-oh. The tone of her voice told him all he needed to know. She was royally pissed off at him. Well, hell, there wasn't much he could do about that until he gave the matter more thought. What had she expected, pillow talk? Promises of forever after? What happened shouldn't have, but it had and now she was probably all hung up thinking his next move would be to buy a ring. Not very damn likely, even though the intensity of their lovemaking this morning had blown him away. So why did he feel like a first-class jerk?

"If I don't finish repairing the bunkhouse porch soon, somebody's going to fall through a rotten board," he explained. "Hutch already stumbled on one yesterday."

He needed an outlet for his frustration and pounding nails in the porch he was repairing would give him just that. He couldn't very well go around smashing his fist through every wall he passed.

"Well, I don't see why. . . ."

Gracie's argument was interrupted when Rena came out of the kitchen door, a baby in each arm.

"Thought you forgot about dinner," she called. "C'mon in, both of you. I'm ready to start frying the chicken and Gracie can help me."

Whit ducked his head at Gracie's questioning look. "Tell her thanks but I've got work to do," he said and took off in his truck, eager to leave the cross-examination that was making him downright uneasy.

Gracie turned on her heels and marched away to gather her babies in her arms without a second glance at Whit. He knew right then she would never let anything come before her children, especially him. That's the way it should be, he reminded himself. He didn't want to be involved permanently. Not when his own plans for the future were finally beginning to fall into place. Yeah, right.

Gracie helped Rena dish up the chicken while the twins reclined in the bouncy seats the older woman had brought along, compliments of her grandchildren who no longer needed them.

Now that the twins were staying awake more often, Gracie knew a blanket on the floor to play on would soon need to be replaced with a real play pen. One of these days, she hoped to go into the city and shop for baby items. She just hadn't figured out how to get there without asking Whit to take her. The old ranch truck still needed a battery. She mentally added transportation to her Want List. She couldn't depend on Whit and his truck forever and asking a neighbor was out of the question, since the closest one was five miles away.

The little town of Peabody had the necessary formula and diapers at the local grocery store, but Gracie would soon need high chairs and larger size clothing for the twins. Max was gaining weight and both babies had already outgrown most of their tiny sleepers. Their bassinets would soon be too small, too. Maintenance of twins was a double expense, but the double joy of having them was worth any sacrifice Gracie made.

She took the pan of biscuits from the oven and started to arrange them on a plate but stopped when Rena put her hand on Gracie's arm and leaned over to whisper in Gracie's ear.

"Well, are you going to tell me why you were gone all morning or do I have to ask Whit myself?"

The older woman's sharp tongue and lack of subtlety made Gracie cringe, even though she knew the threat was a sham. She had no intention of sharing her personal life with anyone and she had too much on her mind to spend time with explanations.

"We simply went for a ride and forgot the time," Gracie whispered back. "I'm sorry you had Max and Susie for so long. I hope they were good." She shot a furtive glance toward the men.

"Humph! Of course they were good," Rena said, taking the plate of biscuits from Gracie. "They're never any trouble, but I can't say the same for those two old men over there who call themselves wranglers." She jerked her head toward the table where Wes and Hutch were impatiently waiting for dinner to be put on the table. "The only thing they're able to wrangle nowadays is food. They fretted all morning, wondering about you and speculating like two old maids. Now, come on, let's get this food on the table before it gets cold. You can tell me the truth later."

Oh, no! The thought of Wes and Hutch conjuring up imaginary situations involving her and Whit and discussing them with Rena gave Gracie a sudden flush of embarrassment. And now she had to sit at the table with them and try to act calm. "Nothing was wrong," she insisted, again in an emphatic whisper. "Whit took me out to see the views from that creek in the west pasture and we just lost track of time. That's the truth."

Rena gave her an "I-don't-believe-that-for-a-minute" look and marched off.

Gracie's stomach clenched as she took her seat, wondering how she was going to get through the meal.

Whit worked steadily all afternoon, his mood just edgy enough for the hot, sweaty job to pacify his need for an outlet for his pent-up frustration. Pounding nails like he was chopping wood released the tension until his cell phone warbled its familiar ring.

Irritated by the interruption, he grabbed the phone from his belt, checked the number and thanked God for caller ID. The last thing he needed right now was a conversation with his father. He let the call transfer to voice mail and kept pounding.

He was finishing up for the day when the phone alerted him for the second time that he had unopened voice messages.

"Yeah, yeah, I hear you."

He knew if he didn't answer his father's persistent calls soon, the old man might decide to make an appearance to check on his not-so-favorite son. He couldn't let that happen now, so he set the hammer aside, sat down on the chair he'd dragged off the porch and prepared for the worst.

The messages were all the same insistent demands, except for the last one delivered in the older Lovett's emphatic roar.

"Get the hell off your butt, Whit, and get those papers signed by tomorrow or expect a visit from Brody. I don't know what's taking you so long to close one simple deal. Call me."

Whitman Lovett, Jr. had given his ultimatum in no uncertain terms. Whitman Lovett, the Third, didn't give a damn.

Damn Brody, too, since he was clearly the instigator of this conspiracy designed to see Whit screw up this final deal.

One day, for crying out loud! One day was all he had to explain to Gracie why he'd lied to her.

Chapter Ten

"Gracie, have you got some time to spare? There's a matter I need to discuss with you." Whit stood on the back porch of the main house, looking through the kitchen door. Four people stared back at him from where they sat around the wooden kitchen table engaged in a game of dominos.

Whit's stomach churned like a blender full off ice cubes. He felt the chill clear down to his boots.

All afternoon he had carefully weighed every option before he'd finally come to a conclusion. Feeling somewhat relieved that the problem would soon be resolved, he'd showered off the day's accumulation of dust and grime from his carpentry work. Decision made, he donned clean clothes and walked to the main house in the evening twilight before he could change his mind. Now that he was here, he was questioning the wisdom of his choice, but it was too late to turn back.

"Well, don't just stand there gawking," Hutch snapped. "Come on in."

Whit did as he was told, mumbled "Thanks," and stepped just inside the door. Suddenly, he was a kid at boarding school again, called into the principal's office to explain his latest prank. The same distress at having no one on his side back then appeared again tonight like a reoccurring toothache.

Gracie cocked her head to one side, studied him intently. "I haven't put the babies to bed yet. Can't it wait until tomorrow?"

"I'd rather not. I can wait while you tuck the little ones in." He couldn't wait and take a chance Brody would show up. "Please?"

"Go ahead, Gracie," Rena coaxed. "We can see to the twins. It's about their bedtime anyway."

Gracie hesitated, then said, "Let me grab a sweater then." She hurried down the hall.

"Thanks. I won't keep her out long," Whit said. He didn't know why he felt he had to explain, but when all three nodded their approval, he figured he'd done the right thing. If only Gracie's approval would be as easy to obtain.

When she returned to the kitchen, Whit's breath caught in his throat at the way she looked.

She'd tied her auburn hair back with a green ribbon that matched her eyes. The glimmer in them caused a tightness in Whit's groin that was impossible to ignore. Deep breathing didn't help much, either.

She'd traded her faded jeans and knit top for a sheer lavender skirt that fell in wispy folds around her pink-toed bare feet and a silky top with skinny straps and a shower of tiny purple flowers on the front. To Whit, she looked like a fairy princess, not the mother of twins and definitely not a rancher. If she'd dressed that way just for him, it made what he was about to do the hardest thing he'd faced in all his thirty-two years.

Dreading the moment but knowing he was doing the right thing, he reached for Gracie's hand as she came down the steps. "Come on, let's walk," he said. "I have something important to tell you."

Gracie followed Whit down the walk and across the yard. She was nervous, wondering what he had to say to her. Another apology? She wasn't sure she could take that. If he said he was sorry they'd made love, she'd die of humiliation. What else could it be? Neither had spoken since he dropped her off after their ride that morning, but she hoped against hope he'd tell her tonight that he planned to stay around a while longer.

Anticipation zipped through her body like an out-of-control locomotive at warp speed. She could barely control her pounding heart.

The feelings she had for Whit had surfaced too soon, but she was ready to accept whatever time they could spend together. At least, she hoped she was. It was premature to think she might really be in love with him. Too soon to expect him to care for her in the same way, even though she'd caught herself imagining how it might be to have his unconditional love.

Still, she'd never forget what they'd shared this morning by the creek. Something so special, she'd kept it close to her heart, re-lived it a thousand times. She wanted to tell him that, let him know how he made her feel when they were together, but it was too soon. So she'd wait until later. Until she was sure whether he intended to stay on the ranch or leave.

They walked along the path, silence accompanying them. Any other time, Gracie would have savored the time alone with Whit, but tonight she knew whatever he had on his mind must be important. She'd felt it ever since their silent ride home from the creek.

At first, she'd feared he regretted making love with her, but she was convinced now that he'd been giving serious thought to their relationship. Why else would he want to talk to her in private? Her heart skipped a beat in anticipation.

A dim light shone through the window of the bunkhouse as they approached the low-roofed building.

"Who could possibly be in the bunkhouse now?" Gracie broke the silence. "Wes and Hutch stayed back at the house to play dominos with Rena after dinner."

Whit stared at the light and for the first time in his life, an anger so explosive he feared he might do something irrational overrode his good sense. Brody! It had to be him, but how had that arrogant bastard slipped into Whit's private territory?

It was all Whit could do to keep his voice calm. "I must've forgotten to turn off the light." Quickly, he blocked Gracie's view with his body, steering her away from the building, but not before he saw the familiar silhouette at the window. He couldn't let her find out Brody was here at Castle Ranch.

She stopped short, looked at him quizzically. "Don't you want to go in and turn it off?"

No, he didn't. "I'll get it later," he muttered. If he went in there now, he was likely to smash his fist into his brother's face.

His plan had been to sit with Gracie on the chairs he'd moved from the bunkhouse porch tonight while he tried to explain matters, but with his brother waiting inside to blow everything to hell and back, Whit knew he'd have to resort to Plan B now. Trouble was, he didn't have a Plan B.

The inevitable couldn't be put off any longer. Very soon, Gracie would know he'd lied and send him packing. So much for careful planning.

"Whit," Gracie persisted, "what is so important you couldn't wait until tomorrow to tell me? And why can't we sit on the porch? I know women aren't allowed in the ranch hands' quarters, but couldn't you make an exception just this once?"

Confusion and disbelief clouded Gracie's face when he said "No." Guilt immediately tied his gut in a knot, but it was too late to back out now. He had to get this mess over with and get back to the bunkhouse before Brody came looking for him.

"I, uh, haven't finished all the repairs yet, so it wouldn't be safe," he said, hoping his lame excuse sounded convincing. "Let's head over to the barn and check on Junior while we talk."

"I'd rather not," Gracie said, slowing her steps. "I don't want to be away from Max and Susie too long. They need to be fed before they go down for a nap and I hate to ask Rena to watch them again, even though she offered."

The tension in the air right then contained enough electricity to give a full-blown Texas heat-lightning storm some stiff competition. The force of it zapped Whit square between the eyes. If he didn't make things right with Gracie tonight, he never would.

"I won't keep you long," he promised. "C'mon, let's just sit over there." He motioned to an old wooden bench leaning against the barn and hurried to dust the cobwebs away with his bandana before they sat.

Gracie perched on the edge of the seat, poised to run if Whit read the stiffness of her posture correctly. Her skirt fell around her legs and skimmed the tops of her sandaled feet. For some damned reason, the sight of her toes peeking out from under those lavender wisps of fabric sent a hot spear of desire coursing through his already electrified body. With more self-control than he thought he possessed, he stifled the memories of Gracie's passionate and uninhibited lovemaking, but they kept coming back, despite his efforts at self-control.

He eased down on the bench next to her, careful to leave some space between them. He didn't dare touch her now, or he'd be a goner. He wouldn't be able to keep from kissing her one last time.

With one final moment of deep regret, Whit turned to admit his disgrace to the woman who'd become more important to him than he'd ever dreamed. The woman who'd captured his heart when he wasn't looking and now held it in her hands. When she tossed it away, as he knew she would, the pain of losing her would hurt like hell. He wasn't sure he could survive it.

"I lied to you, Gracie. Lied about everything." He held his breath. She would hate him now, he was certain. How could she not?

"I don't understand," she said, frowning.

"I'm not who I said I was. My real name is Whitman Carter Lovett, and I'm not a cowboy. Never worked on a ranch in my life. Maybe you've heard of Lovett Geological Survey. That's my father's company in Texas City. There's also a branch office in San Antonio. The business is highly successful in locating underground natural gas." He looked away, anticipating the censure in her eyes. "I was sent here to make a deal for leasing your land. Meeting you by accident like I did was a lucky break for me. Hiring me gave me the opportunity to check out the entire lay of the land and see if it met the needs of our company."

There, he'd said it. He swallowed hard to dispel the bitter taste in his mouth left by his confession. The fist squeezing his heart made it almost impossible to breathe.

Gracie stared at him, wide-eyed. "You only wanted my land?" Her lips trembled as she spoke. "You made love with me to get my ranch? How could you, Whit? How could you?" Her voice, barely a whisper at first, rose sharply as the full impact of Whit's admission began to settle in her brain.

She jumped up to leave, but before she did, she looked him straight in the eyes. "Did you have so little respect for me you thought I could be bought? I wish I'd never met you, Whit Lovett."

Tears streamed down her face and stung her eyes as she fled for the safety of the house. Her heart had cracked when she first listened to Whit's unbelievable admission, but now it splintered into a million jagged pieces. Mortified, deeply hurt and angry beyond belief, she wanted to pound her fists into his chest, hurt him like he'd hurt her. She wanted him to remember the sweetness of their kisses, their passionate joining when they'd skyrocketed together in exquisite completion and know that he'd never have her that way again.

She'd given Whit her total trust, along with her heart, and he'd betrayed her, lied to her. What a fool she'd been to think she'd found love at last. Just because a good-looking cowboy talked her into having sex. And, she painfully acknowledged, that's all it had been to him, just a moment of hot, sweaty sex to satisfy his male needs. There'd been no love involved on his part, even though his actions and whispered words had been convincing at the time. He'd used her and she wondered how she could have been so naïve.

"Gracie, wait!" Whit came after her, caught her hands and pulled her into his arms. "Please, there's so much more to explain. Even a criminal gets a chance to plead his case."

She jerked free from his embrace. "You had your chance," she said through her tears, then left him standing in the path.

She ran up the back steps and burst into the room. Just as Gracie expected, Rena was seated at the long oak table with Wes and Hutch, dominoes still spread out in the center of it. But the sandy-haired stranger seated in the fourth chair stopped her in her tracks. She waited, heart racing, for her friends to explain. The wait wasn't long, but the explanation was totally unexpected.

The man stood and extended his hand to Gracie. "You must be Gracie Castle. I'm Brody Lovett, Whit's brother."

She gathered her composure and shook his hand. "Are you looking for Whit, Mr. Lovett?" She hadn't even known he had a brother. What else had Whit lied about besides his name? "I think you'll find him in the bunkhouse."

Brody shrugged. "Actually, I came to see you, as well, Ms. Castle." He pulled out his chair for Gracie, and when she took it, he pulled another chair next to hers and took some papers from a black leather briefcase lying on the table. "It's about the lease agreement."

He was nothing like Whit, Gracie noted. His manners were perfect, the timbre of his voice was as soft as the hand she accepted with reluctance. His impeccable appearance shouted "money". No worn, faded jeans or dusty boots for this Lovett son. But it was the coldness in his eyes that sent shivers skittering along Gracie's spine.

Whit yanked open the door to his bunkhouse quarters and barreled into the room ready to punch his brother's lights out. He swore loudly at the empty room. He stomped across the room to the bathroom, slammed the door when he discovered no one there, either.

"Dammit, Brody, where are you?" His angry shout ricocheted off the bunkhouse walls.

Whatever reason Brody had for showing up unannounced, Whit wasn't about to let his money-hungry sibling cheat Gracie out of her own right to drill on her land. Not before he had a chance to explain his own plan. To hell with the company. Gracie needed his help. And his gut tightened when he realized he needed Gracie.

Right now, she hated the sight of him, but he knew that with a little more time, he could make her understand. He couldn't let Brody screw up everything. But that's what would happen if Gracie discovered his brother here. Time. He needed more time.

With one last angry glance around the room, Whit left the bunkhouse and hurried to the main house. He hoped to hell Brody hadn't beaten him there.

The scene in the kitchen when Whit burst through the door sent his heart plummeting straight to his boots. Brody sat next to Gracie, leaning close and talking in that soft, have-I-got-a-deal-for-you tone that Whit had heard too many times.

Gracie's pale face was pinched, and Whit could tell she'd been crying. Her eyes were red-rimmed and damp. His first reaction was to rearrange his brother's perfect face with a well-placed fist. Instead, he grabbed Brody by his arm and pulled him out of his chair.

"Excuse us a minute," he said to the others, then propelled Brody toward the door.

Brody shook loose from his angry brother's grasp, tugged his tailor-made shirt back in place and gave Whit a look of contempt. The other occupants of the room held their breath and sat still as statues.

When Whit had Brody on the porch safely out of hearing distance of the kitchen, he cut loose.

"Just what do you think you're doing here, Brody? Didn't I tell you to stay out of my business?"

"I'm merely tying up some loose ends regarding the lease," Brody answered. "If you'd listened to me in the first place, everything would have been done by now and Ms. Castle would have a nice bit of money in her bank account. However, since you obviously let your personal feelings get in the way of your obligations to the company, Dad sent me to clean up after you." This isn't the first time I've had to save your hide."

Whit locked his jaw to keep from spouting words not fit for mixed company. "I'll give you two minutes to grab your briefcase and apologize to Gracie," he said, after he'd gained control of his anger enough to speak. "Two minutes, Brody, that's all."

Then he pushed his sibling back into the kitchen.

"Brody was just leaving," Whit said, sweeping the papers from the table into Brody's briefcase. "His offer's just been dropped."

"No!" Gracie jumped up, surprising everyone. "It's my ranch and I say he can stay, at least until I hear everything he has to say. If there's a way to make this place profitable, I want to hear it and Mr. Brody Lovett's offer sounds like it could be the answer to my predicament. Sit down and be quiet or leave, Whit."

Brody nodded, a satisfied smirk on his face. "Thank you, Ms. Castle," he said, oozing charm wasted on his audience. "I appreciate your patience and understanding."

Before he took his place again beside Gracie, he turned to Whit. "Now, if you'll excuse us, big brother, the lady and I have business to discuss."

Gracie's face was drained of all expression, her movements stiff and awkward when she sat down again. Whit made a move toward Brody, but Wes pushed his chair away from the table. His arthritic fingers gripped Whit's arm, surprising Whit with their strength.

"Fightin' ain't gonna solve anything, son," he said quietly. "Gracie's right. It's her decision whether your brother stays or goes. Fact is, you shoulda' told her up front about that lease offer and who you really were. It don't bode well to hide the truth. Now, why don't you mosey on back to the bunkhouse and leave this matter to Gracie? Me 'n Hutch will be along directly."

Ever the peace-maker, Wes tried to push Whit toward the door, but Whit refused to budge from where he had his boots firmly planted on the kitchen floor.

"I'm not going anywhere until I hear my brother's entire proposal." There was no mistaking Whit meant what he said.

Wes cast a questioning look in Gracie's direction, but kept his hand firmly around Whit's arm.

After an awkward silence, Gracie nodded. "All right. You may stay as long as you don't interrupt."

"Fine. Whatever you say." Whit gave in, nearly choking on the false promise. If Brody even came close to cheating Gracie, there was no way Whit was going to keep quiet. A plan already forming in his mind, one that could make Gracie the rightful owner of any speculation drilling done on the Castle Ranch. A two-edged plan that could get him fired from the ranch or help him win Gracie's heart. Only time would tell. Either way, it wouldn't be easy, but he had to try.

He'd been too damn slow to realize just how important Gracie and her kids had become to him. He leaned back in his chair, arms crossed defiantly across his chest, while his temper simmered just below boiling point. This was one fight baby brother wasn't going to win, even if Whit had to walk away in order to give Gracie the security she needed for her and the twins. He'd leave if it meant Gracie's happiness, but his heart would remain at Castle Ranch.

Gracie listened to the two brothers' bitter exchange. Had Whit truly meant to deceive her when he first arrived at the ranch? She wanted to believe his reasons were honest ones, but how could she, if his brother was telling the truth?

What she'd heard of Brody's offer so far, made her wonder why Whit was opposed to her leasing her land. The money she'd make would help with her ever-growing expenses. She could buy a decent vehicle, maybe even purchase a few more head of cattle to add to Hercules' harem. Why wouldn't he want that for her?

She'd lived on the ranch long enough now to realize she wanted to stay in Texas and make the Castle ranch her home. The thought of becoming a productive rancher appealed to her for many reasons, most importantly to give Max and Susie a chance to grow up in the serene security of the Hill Country. She'd finally found a place to belong. A place where she could give them so much more than she could have in her tiny Minneapolis apartment. Why shouldn't she let the Lovett Company lease her land? Why did Whit disagree so adamantly?

"The bottom line, Ms. Castle, is if you permit our company to lease your land, you'll get to keep the initial payment whether we hit a productive vein of gas or not. If we're lucky, and I'm quite sure we'll be, you'll get a percentage of the production royalties after that." Brody Lovett named a figure that staggered Gracie, even as a possibility. His air of confidence was so convincing, Gracie couldn't imagine him not finding whatever he was looking for.

"And you're positive a gas vein runs through my property?"

Brody's paused for a second to clear his throat. "Well, of course, we only have our geological maps, but our studies have a sterling record of success. And as I said, we'll pay you handsomely for the chance to do the exploration at our expense."

Gracie saw Whit scowl at his brother's words and felt an ache of regret. But she wouldn't give in to her pain. This was a chance to get the ranch back on its feet. She would take Brody's offer and build her home alone. No, she corrected, not alone. She had Max and Susie, as well as Wes and Hutch. Her family. That would have to be enough.

But loneliness remained a constant companion to her broken heart.

"I'll consider your offer carefully and let you know tomorrow, Mr. Lovett, uh, Brody." She avoided Whit's eyes. "I'll look over the contract tonight."

Brody thanked her, shook hands with her as well as Wes and Hutch, and with a smug, "See how simple it is to get the job done, big brother?" he left.

Gracie watched Whit stride after him. "Do you think they'll wind up fighting?" She'd never seen this angry side of Whit. Of course, what did she really know about Whit Lovett, after all?

"Naw," Hutch said. "They won't fight. That citified younger brother is too concerned with keeping his fancy duds all proper-like to take on a scrapper like Whit. And, didja' see those lily-white hands? That feller wouldn't take a chance on getting them dirty. Besides, Whit's too decent to hit any man too weak to defend hisself"

"True," Wes agreed with a nod of his head. "Those two are as different as horses and cows."

"Whatcha' gonna' do, Gracie?" Hutch asked. "The money sounds good, but it don't seem like Whit cottons to the idea, even though it's his daddy's company giving the offer."

"I'm not going to decide anything right now," Gracie said. "I need to check on Max and Susie. I can hear them fussing in their bassinets and if I don't get to them soon, they'll be too wound up to go back to sleep. I'll study the contract later."

After Gracie left, Rena began putting away the dominoes without asking her playing partners whether they wanted to continue the game or not.

Wes hem-hawed around, pretending to help while giving the last of the pecan-topped chocolate cake a wishful glance.

"A last cup of coffee would sure go good with a piece of that cake, Rena."

"It would?" she said, acting like she didn't know what Wes was hinting for. She retrieved the pan of chocolate decadence from the counter with a sly smile. "Then I'll make a fresh pot. And Wesley Paxton, you keep your fingers out of that frosting."

Over coffee and cake, the trio hashed over the events of the evening, determined to help Gracie make the right choice.

Chapter Eleven

In the bedroom, Gracie pulled the soft, pink sheet up to cover little Susie's tummy, smoothing the tufts of downy, pale hair on the baby's head. Max made little baby noises. She marveled at the peaceful way they slept, content and secure in their new world.

"I don't think I could have given you up if I had known how easy it would be to love you two," she whispered to her tiny munchkins. They were so much a precious part of her life now. She couldn't imagine life without them.

Sadly, the wonderful experience of being a mother would never have been Gracie's if it hadn't been for the tragic accident that took the lives of the intended parents. She'd chosen to sign their contract and take their money in exchange for carrying these precious babies for them. Remembering it all brought an ache in her heart and a fresh flood of tears to her eyes.

Guilt tangled with duty in Gracie's conscience. Was her heart so callous she'd felt no sympathy when she'd learned the babies' grandfather was physically unable to care for the children? No, even though at first she'd been resentful at being trapped in a situation she hadn't wanted. She remembered the excitement she felt at the prospect of finally having the opportunity to think only of her needs, her future. Selfish, maybe, but she'd carried the weight of responsibility for her mother's care for so long, she didn't want anything to prevent her from achieving the independence she'd longed for and planned for. Even sacrificed for.

With the initial payment for her part in the surrogacy, Gracie had managed to pay all her mother's medical bills and still have a little left over for herself. Adding two babies to her newly-acquired independence had definitely not been part of her plans. Neither was moving to Texas. She knew nothing about raising children, aside from watching her own mother fail miserably at it. The thought of becoming a full-time mother scared her to death. Having no choice angered her.

Then she met Whit, had the babies, found out she liked living in the Texas Hill Country in spite of the two old men who still made her feel not-quite-adequate as a Texan. But most surprising of all was how she fell head-over-heels in love with Max and Susie, something she hadn't expected, at all.

Now, all she wanted was to be able to provide for her new family, and that included Wes, Hutch and even Rena, in a comfortable and secure environment. Leasing her land was the sensible thing to do.

Falling for Whit Lovett was completely unexpected and if she could undo what had already transpired between them, she would do so in a heartbeat. Only the fact that she still needed Whit's help on the ranch kept her from sending him packing earlier. Being around him every day was tantamount to being subjected to a temptation too great to ignore.

Could she survive if Whit walked out when he learned her decision? She knew Wes and Hutch could always provide her with moral support, but Whit had been the one to tackle the chores requiring his physical strength. She'd gradually come to depend on his ability to take charge of ranch matters, leaving the weightier decisions to him. That was a mistake she'd have to remedy. Running the ranch without him meant learning every aspect of the business, but she could—and would do it. She'd put aside her own wants and desires and concentrate on her children and the family she'd come to love. And she'd do it without Whit Lovett.

She picked up the contract and settled in the rocking chair next to the cribs, determined to study every clause and weigh every option before she made her final decision that would affect the future of everyone she loved, even Whit.

She must've dozed, because it was after midnight when the ache in her neck awakened her. Yawning, she rolled her shoulders to work out the kinks.

She peeked at the sound asleep tots to make sure they were settled for the night, then tiptoed out of the room, making a side trip to the bathroom before getting ready for bed.

The unsettling events of the evening had taken their toll, physically and emotionally. She didn't want to lie awake with wordy contract clauses, along with painful images of Whit's angry face running around in her mind.

She turned on the faucets in the old, claw-footed tub and added a few drops of the lavender-scented bath oil she'd found on her grandmother's dressing table. A relaxing bath was exactly what she needed to soothe her troubled soul.

Her mind was still boggled by all the papers Brody Lovett had given her. She'd studied them as best she could, not always understanding the legal terms, but confident that what Brody offered was above and beyond anything Whit could ever do to help her do to make the ranch profitable.

She stepped into the tub, sliding under the fragrant bubbles until all but her head was immersed in the water's soothing warmth. Sighing, she leaned against the back of the tub, closed her eyes, and forced herself to relax. She wanted to forget for a moment all the problems facing her. The choices she must make between accepting Brody's offer and trying to understand Whit's reasons why she shouldn't. The choice was hers. But how would she know if she'd made the right one?

Whether it was the scent of her grandmother's lavender bath oil or simply the relaxing warmth of the water that helped Gracie's nerves unwind, she wasn't certain, but when she left the bathroom forty-five minutes later, she knew what her decision would be.

Holding a frayed, white towel around her damp body with one hand and rubbing her freshly-shampooed hair with another, she padded barefoot down the hall to her bedroom. She had just pulled her knit pajama top over her head, when a tiny cry came from the children's bedroom. She shoved her arms the rest of the way through the sleeves, then tugged on the bottoms. With the towel wrapped turban-style around her hair, she made her way to the twin's room.

Moonlight lit the narrow hallway, but by now, Gracie could have found the way to her babies' room blindfolded. She hurried, her bare feet barely making a sound on the wooden planked floor. She started to call out, but the sobs halted abruptly, and she slowed her steps.

Whit's shadowed figure stood by Susie's crib, rocking back and forth as he crooned softly to the whimpering baby cradled in his arms. Gracie stepped back from the doorway and listened with her heart.

Whit's slightly off-key voice was gruffly tender as he serenaded her tiny daughter with words to a tune she'd never heard. But what caused the unbearable ache of longing deep in her soul was more than the lyrics of the lullaby. When she saw the raw emotion he'd kept hidden for so long, now unashamedly exposed by the silent tears dampening his face, all her anger and doubts melted away.

"Hush, little baby, let me sing you a song
Of a cowboy's heart that will always belong
To you and your momma. I promise my love
'Til stars cry their sad tears from heaven above."

Gracie spun around and braced herself against the wall, all the breath in her body suddenly stilled. What was he doing? Why had he come back?

Whit had never shown much interest in the twins, outside of an occasional inquiry about their general health. Never acted like he cared about children at all. Would he have wanted children, if they'd married? How little she really knew about the real man singing a lullaby to her daughter.

She didn't know what had brought him back to the house or what had prompted him to try to soothe her crying baby, but as much as she wanted to confront him, as much as she longed for his touch, she had to slip away before he saw her. Before she found herself in his arms, which was exactly what would happen if she walked into the room right now.

She needed more time to search her heart to find the answers she needed and the strength to forgive this man who loved her. The man she loved more than she'd ever thought possible.

Heavy footsteps sounded outside her room before she could slip into her bed. Her heart pounded when Whit stopped in the doorway, hands at his sides, dark eyes glistening with tears.

"I knew you were there." His rough whisper floated across the silent room.

Gracie nodded as she inched away from the bed. She didn't want to be anywhere near Whit or a bed at the moment. Her head whirled with memories of the last time they'd been together. The images were indelibly burned in her mind forever. This wasn't the time to let her emotions rule her head. She had to think of her children, not her heart.

"Why did you come back?"

He ran shaky hands through his hair, shook his head and walked slowly across the room, stopping only inches in front of her. The woodsy fragrance of aftershave and the freshly-showered scent of Irish Spring on his skin enveloped her, teased her, tempted her.

His dark eyes searched her face, lingered for a heated moment on her mouth, then moved lower in a visual caress so sensual, so intimate, every sensitive part of Gracie's body ached for his touch.

"I came back to try one more time to talk you out of taking Brody's offer. You were in the shower and Susie was fussing, so I picked her up. I hadn't intended for you to see me." His gaze locked with hers.

She took a step back, needing to put some space between them before she burst into flames. The uncontrollable desire that flared inside her every time Whit came near was too much to deal with right now. She had absolutely no shame when it came to loving Whit.

"Thank you for putting Susie back to sleep. I don't think there's any more to say between us. My decision is made." She kept her voice calm, distant, in spite of the earthquake rocking her insides. She couldn't let him know how he'd touched her heart with his lullaby. Not yet.

For a long moment, Whit stood unmoving, studying her face intently before he spoke.

"Then I guess this is goodbye." He closed the space between them, dipped his head and touched his lips to hers, then turned away. "The pleasure was always all mine, Ms. Castle," he said and walked out of the door without a backward glance.

The back door slammed. Heartsick, Gracie wondered if he'd be gone tomorrow. Wondered why she'd let him go.

A long time later, sleep finally came to her rescue.

The parade of heavy equipment being hauled across the field on an assortment of trucks and trailers kicked up a cloud of Texas dust as far as Gracie could see. Max and Susie had awakened earlier than usual and she'd gotten up to feed them. Now she stood on the porch holding a baby in each arm, squinting into the morning sun as the Lovett team clanged and bumped their way to the drilling site.

"Look, sweethearts, they're here." The babies squirmed their disinterest and Gracie readjusted them on her hips, pleased at their steady weight gain, yet a little sad knowing it wouldn't be too long before they'd be too big for her to carry them both at the same time. Cuddle time with them was her favorite time of day.

Susie wiggled, fussing her discomfort, so Gracie put the two in their new playpen and gave them each a soft toy to play with. Susie ignored the pink bunny, preferring to stick her fingers in her mouth instead, but Max immediately let out an unhappy howl when his brown fuzzy teddy bear bounced beyond his reach. Gracie gave Max a tummy tickle before she rolled the toy back, then settled down in one of the padded porch rockers to enjoy the morning breeze and continued to watch the line of trucks go by like an army of ants.

The sight of so much activity made Gracie wince. The entire ranch had begun to change. Getting used to it was taking some serious effort on her part. The biggest change was having to cope without Whit.

He'd left the ranch the morning after she'd heard his heartfelt rendition of the lullaby he sang to Susie. It was difficult for Gracie to let go of the hurt she felt by his betrayal. She didn't know if she could ever forgive him for lying about his identity. Trust wasn't something she gave easily and Whit had jeopardized that trust by his own doing. Losing him had broken her heart, but she'd lived with disappointment before and she could do it again. Having little Max and Susie to love made up for any heartache she'd experienced in the three weeks since the unexpected appearance of Brody Lovett turned her life upside down. Signing the lease agreement with LGS had caused her almost as much anxiety as her decision to sign the surrogate contract. She hoped her decision was the right one.

With the initial check from the Lovett Company safely deposited in the local bank, she could breathe a little easier. From now on, life at the Castle ranch would be much easier for everyone, except Whit.

She thought about Whit and how he'd avoided her since she'd signed the deal with Brody. He'd left the ranch as she'd expected, but surprised her by coming back two days later.

He avoided her, though, arriving for meals after everyone else had finished, often taking his plate back to the bunkhouse. He was always polite to Rena, complimenting her on her cooking, but he never stayed to talk with Gracie or play with the babies.

Gracie didn't know if he talked to Wes and Hutch or not, but supposed he did because he'd kept on working, just as he'd been hired to do in the beginning. No chore went undone, not even around the house. He'd even found a way to keep the unruly chickens from escaping their coop and roosting on the front porch.

He'd given her no clue why he was still around, didn't even ask if she wanted him there, which was a good thing because every time she saw him, her heart beat a little faster. She'd had to give his paycheck to Wes to deliver. Whit never cashed it, leaving her more frustrated than ever. Did he think he was indispensable? That she was incompetent?

When she remembered how he'd lied to her, the tiny crack in her heart grew wider, letting anger fill the empty space where love had just begun to grow. Trust was important and Whit had betrayed hers. Singing a lullaby to her daughter didn't pardon his crime of betrayal. The tender side of Whit that she'd discovered wasn't enough to mend the hole in her heart. Almost, but not quite.

Her mood swings lately went from disappointment to aching loneliness to stubborn resolve and back again. Only when Whit was no longer in the picture would she be able to move forward.

As the last of the parade of equipment disappeared beyond the horizon and the dust from their rattling wheels settled over the land she had come to love, Gracie accepted the only solution that could save her ranch . . . and her heart. Whit Lovett had to go.

Whit parked his truck close to the barn and got out. He could see Gracie and the babies from a safe distance behind the steady stream of trucks, his heart heavy with regret.

He hadn't been able to stop the progress Brody had made since acquiring Gracie's signature on the lease document, so Whit had buried himself in ranch work instead. Doing his best not to think about her was damn near impossible since she occupied his thoughts both day and night. Especially the night.

Every time he closed his eyes she was there. Memories of how he'd held her in his arms, kissed her sweet lips and loved her the way a woman deserved to be loved brought an unrelenting ache of longing. Why hadn't he told her how he felt?

Watching his brother puff up like a toad and use his silver-tongued powers of persuasion to convince Gracie she was making the right choice had whipped Whit's anger to a dangerous level. Brody didn't care about anyone but himself. Never had. Never would.

But, wait a minute! Wasn't he as unscrupulous as his little brother? In the beginning, his only consideration had been for what *he* hoped to gain—a total break from the Lovett enterprises so he could buy his dream ranch and live his own life as he pleased. Yeah, he'd been totally selfish in a lot of ways. He knew that now, but it was too late for regrets.

The offer he'd been prepared to make would've been much higher and fair. Gracie would've been a lot better off if he'd simply told her the truth right at first. Stalling for time had only hurt her instead of helping her. Deceiving Gracie about his true identity had worked against him. No wonder she hated him.

Whit didn't know if he'd ever earn her trust again, but one thing was certain. He would stay at the ranch until he was damn sure Brody's venture paid off for Gracie. And if it failed he intended to be around to pick up the pieces if she'd let him.

"What in tarnation you doin' hiding back here?"

At the sound of the gravelly voice, Whit spun around so fast he whacked his elbow on the door handle of the truck. Hutch and Wes stood behind him, close enough for Whit to see the wrinkles in their leathery faces and catch a whiff of the coffee they constantly consumed.

"Dammit, that's a good way to get cold-cocked," he said, rubbing his injured arm. The mood he was in, they were lucky he hadn't taken a swing at them. "Next time, holler before you sneak up like that."

Both men eyed him warily. Hutch repeated his question, but before Whit could answer, Wes proceeded to shake a knobby finger at him.

"Appears to me you're the one being sneaky," Wes said. "Who you hidin' from?"

Whit rolled his eyes. "I'm not hiding from anyone or anything. Just watching the drilling equipment coming in, that's all."

"Looks to me like you're watching Gracie without letting her see you. In my book that's hiding."

"Yeah, or stalking," Hutch added, a scowl knitting his gray eyebrows together across the deep creases in his forehead.

"Oh, for cryin' out loud, do I look like a stalker?" Whit continued to nurse his aching elbow and tried not to appear as unnerved as he felt by the men's accusations. They hadn't been overly friendly since they'd found out his identity.

"Not so sure what one looks like, but I do know you've been acting mighty strange lately." Hutch cleared his throat. "You know, Lovett, what's done is done so you might as well get used to it. Gracie made her choice for the good of the ranch and we're thinking she made a good'un. I'm just surprised she ain't sent you packing yet."

He paused, his gaze darting from Whit's scowling face to Gracie sitting on the back porch, then back to Whit, before he continued. "You ain't too happy with that brother of yours, are you? Could that be on account of you wanted Gracie to be beholden to you and not Brody? Or does what's causing you grief go deeper than that?"

The question sucker-punched Whit right where it mattered—in his conscience. Was he that obvious? The oldsters were digging too deep, getting too close to his personal space. He wanted to tell them to take a hike for fear they'd discover the truth. His private emotions weren't for public discussion.

To Whit's relief, good ol' Hutch took that moment to expound the virtues of truth and honesty, so Whit managed to avoid answering Wes's probing cross-examination without being disrespectful.

Whit listened to the tirade, knowing if he didn't, he was pretty sure the old boys would make a bee-line to the house to tell Gracie. He was beginning to believe the old-timers were more perceptive than he gave them credit for. They both had a tendency to gossip at meal time. It wouldn't do for Gracie to get wind of the real reason Whit was still around. He wasn't ready to walk away from the situation yet. Not until he made sure Gracie had everything she needed to get along without his help.

"Well, if you ain't spying on her, why don't you go on over there and set a spell? Gracie's been asking how come you don't eat with us no more." Wes kept on harping.

Whit glowered right back. "And face her wrath? I'm not that dumb, even if I did screw up things right from the get-go."

"You got that right, Lovett. You made a real mess of things. And lately, you've been moping around like a sorrowful-faced hound dog. Me'n Hutch may be old, but we ain't blind. We see the way you look at her when nobody's watching. Never figured you for a quitter, though. Thought you'd be in there making things right with the gal."

"Quitter? You think I'm a quitter? Hell, what was I supposed to do? I told her the truth. She's got every right to despise me, Wes. Every right."

Hutch took hold of Whit's arm, looked him in the eye. "You're dumber than a box of rocks, Lovett, if you think she feels that way. Sure, she'll deny it if you ask, but the gal's got a real soft spot in her heart where you're concerned. Like I said, we ain't blind. What you have to remember, though, is a woman's got pride. Their feelings are tender and you have to treat them careful like. With respect. You can't just sweet talk 'em, then walk away. Not if you expect to win them over. Right, Wes?"

Hutch's white head bobbed up and down in agreement. "Yep, and unless you want to wind up with nothing but the tail lights of that truck of yours shining in her face, you have to let her know you care. You do, don't you?"

The old man's stern look was hard for Whit to ignore. He rubbed a hand over his face. That was one loaded question he wasn't about to answer. Instead, he fired one of his own back at the pair.

"How'd you two learn so much about women?" Sometimes, offense is the best defense.

Red-faced, Hutch stared at the ground, but Wes showed no such discomfort. "Lovett, a man can't live long enough to learn everything there is to know about women, but me and Hutch sure had us some good times doin' our homework on the subject," Wes said with a wink. "Someday, Gracie'll find her grandma's journal and figure out the rest of the Castle history. If you're lucky, she'll share it with you. Then the two of you can take up where me and Hutch left off. That's all I'm gonna say."

He gave Whit a shove toward his truck. "Now get going before that sneaky brother of yours beats you to it. I've got a hunch he's after more than just Gracie's ranch land."

"You're right, but there's not much I can do about it now." Whit had the same feeling ever since he'd seen Brody's head bent close to Gracie's at the kitchen table, but he hadn't wanted to acknowledge it. Hearing Wes say the words out loud made the knot sitting in his gut burn like he'd eaten a jar full of jalapenos.

"The hell there ain't!" Wes and Hutch both exploded in chorus at the same time.

Hutch stopped sputtering long enough to send Whit a withering look along with a piece of advice. "You can do anything you put your mind to, if you want to bad enough. That gal back there on the porch is hurtin' and you're the only one who can fix that. If you don't aim to try, then it's time to get your carcass off the Castle property and let her get on with running the ranch and raising her kids. She's got money now, thanks to your brother." He took off his hat and scratched his head. "Come to think of it, mebbe you don't deserve her, after all." He jammed his hat down on his head so hard his ears pushed out like wings.

Every one of the old cowboy's sharp words was a well-aimed bullet, but Whit was damned if he'd willingly stand in the line of fire. Before any more bullets could hit their mark, he was in back his truck, wheels spinning down the dirt track toward the house.

His mind on everything but his driving, Whit swerved sharply, barely missing an armadillo lying in the road. Thoughts about Gracie and the rotten way he'd deceived her crowded his brain. He'd fully expected to her to send him packing sooner.

When he'd left the day after Gracie had caught him acting all sloppy and sentimental over a baby's lullaby, he hadn't intended to come back. But after he'd taken care of some business, he had returned. Gracie and her babies were the only bright spot in his life. He knew it was time for him to leave permanently, but he couldn't leave without telling her how he felt.

None of the dreams he'd built around his own future mattered now. Dreams of putting down roots far away from the Lovett family compound on a ranch of his own with a home he'd crafted with his own hands weren't worth the effort, if he had no one to share it with him.

Yet, the dreams lingered, hidden in that special corner of his heart reserved only for secret longings.

For the last three nights, Gracie's appearance in his private dreams had rocked him to the core. That's when he knew his life would be empty without her and her babies.

Whit jammed his foot on the accelerator harder, sending the truck flying faster down the rutted road. His thoughts were on Gracie and the twins. He had to get back while she was still on the porch. He'd beg if he had to, but he needed to tell her she was the only dream that mattered. He prayed he'd get there in time to tell her he loved her.

When the tires hit a washed-out rut and the truck careened sideways down the dirt road, it was too late to avoid the giant oak tree that had the audacity to be right in his way.

He yanked the wheel, but two seconds wasn't enough. That's all the time he had before the air bag exploded. Hours later, he woke up in a hospital bed with the mother of all headaches.

Chapter Twelve

Gracie perched on the edge of a nearby chair, staring intently at the man in the hospital bed as she'd done the last four hours. The man who had burst into her life and captured her heart, then shattered it with lies.

When Whit's younger brother had been overbearingly solicitous after the crash, offering to hire another ranch hand to take Whit's place. She'd argued vehemently that Whit was still an employee because he hadn't given his notice and she hadn't fired him. Brody was certain Whit was planning to leave and told her so.

Gracie silently hoped he was wrong. Even though she might never be able to trust him again, she didn't want Whit to leave. Not yet. Not until she figured out why. She couldn't even explain her reason for sitting here at his bedside, when Wes or Hutch could've stayed just as easily.

Her initial anger and confused emotions over the situation with Whit had quickly disappeared when the shattering sound of the crash reached the porch and she saw Wes and Hutch hurrying up the path, shouting for her to call 9-1-1.

The rest of the day was a blur. The twins were turned over to Rena. The two old ranch hands drove Gracie to the hospital in the used pickup she'd recently purchased with some of the lease money. The men stayed until they were certain Whit was out of danger, then returned to the ranch to take care of chores.

Gracie insisted on remaining with Whit a while longer. Wes promised to pick her up later after he and Hutch finished chores.

She paced the room, glancing at Whit's still body every minute or two. She knew he needed to rest, but couldn't help hoping he'd wake up before she had to leave.

When the nurse came in to check his vital signs, Whit's eyes slowly fluttered open.

"What-? Owww!" He reached up, felt the bandage on his head and groaned. "What's the other guy look like?"

"You'll have to ask your visitor when I've finished here," the nurse said, sticking the thermometer in his mouth.

Gracie smiled. In spite of the awful accident, Whit had come out of it with only a mild concussion, a couple of bruised ribs and a small cut on his forehead that needed stitches. She was relieved to see his sense of humor hadn't been damaged.

"You're lucky," she told him. "The other guy was a big oak tree that didn't feel a thing. I suggest you avoid him next time, though, in case he's looking for revenge."

Whit managed a crooked grin. "My truck?"

Gracie hated being the bearer of bad news. "I'm sorry, Whit. The truck didn't fare so well. Wes had it towed to the body shop in town. I don't know if they can revive it or not. Your brother said not to worry, he'd take care of the matter."

Whit tried to sit up, but eased back on his pillow with a moan. She reached for the glass of water on his bedside table.

"Here, drink a little of this. The doctor said your ribs were badly bruised and you're going to be sore for two or three weeks."

Whit raised his head and sipped slowly through the straw.

"Thanks." He eased his head back on the pillow and closed his eyes again. "You can tell Brody to butt out," he said, after a moment's pause. "I'll take care of things myself."

"He told me you'd say that."

Whit slowly opened his eyes. Gracie knew that smoldering look. She'd seen it before right before they'd made love. She knew what it meant then, but now she was confused. What did it mean now?

Her reaction to Whit's gaze was the same one that had sent hot spears of need slicing through her body. She rose and walked to the window, breathing deeply until she felt she could control her emotions.

"Your brother was only looking out for me." She knew that wasn't exactly true. She waited expectantly for Whit to deny Brody's statement that he would be leaving soon.

"My brother never looks out for anyone but himself, Gracie. Why do you think we never got along?"

"How would I know that? You never even told me you had a brother. Nothing you ever told me was the truth, was it?"

She knew now was not the time to resurrect the past, but as long as she kept her anger alive, she wouldn't give in to the sudden urge to crawl into bed with Whit and wrap her arms around his aching body.

Silly, she chided herself. Don't be foolish enough to fall for the same old lies. More than ever, she longed for someone she could trust. But she was slowly learning the hard way to trust herself. That's all she needed in order to take care of her ranch and her babies.

She didn't realize she'd been pacing the floor until Whit spoke. With a weary heart, she sat down again, determined to listen no matter how much it hurt or how much she wanted to believe.

"I never intended to lie, Gracie. But I knew you wouldn't let me hire on if you knew I was really a Lovett with a reputation for crooked dealings and money to burn. For some reason I didn't understand then, it was important to me for you to know the man beneath all the society trappings. A man who wanted to help, but not with the influence of his wealth." His voice cracked, raw with emotion, his face reflecting his pain. "A man surprised to learn he cared deeply for an extraordinary woman and her babies. A man deeply ashamed, but not too proud to ask for forgiveness."

Her gaze flew to his face. Did she dare believe him? No. He was still her hired hand. That's why she stayed with him tonight. Not because she cared for him in any other way. No, not that. She couldn't bear to be hurt again.

She clasped her hands tightly in her lap. A fat tear slid down her cheek, landing there before she could brush it away. She couldn't—wouldn't—admit her feelings until her bruised heart healed. And that would never happen without trust.

Brody Lovett's unexpected appearance in the doorway just then gave the turbulent tension filling the room another target. Whit stifled his anger, unwilling to give Gracie more reason for doubting his words.

"What brings you here, Brody? Shouldn't you be out at the site, playing the big boss?" The tone of his voice left no doubt how Whit felt about his younger brother's arrival. "Not your humanitarian good-will, I'll wager. And how'd you find out about the accident?" Despite his effort to stay calm, Whit couldn't keep the bitterness out of his voice.

"Wes and Hutch told me. Those two were pretty upset about what happened, so I got here as soon as I could. I was concerned about you."

Brody's superficial attempt at sympathy set Whit's teeth on edge. "Hoped I'd kicked the bucket, didn't you? Too bad, because I don't even have any broken bones, just some bruises and a few stitches. Guess you lose, little brother." Whit didn't even try to hide the animosity in his voice.

"Whit, what an awful thing to say," Gracie said.

A wave of nausea threatened Whit's stomach. Did he hear her correctly? Had she just sided with his brother? Damn Brody for interrupting when Whit was in the middle of something important. And the conversation with Gracie was more serious now than ever. "I would never wish you dead, Whit," Brody said, his face solemn except for a disarming glint in his gray eyes, "so I'll blame your nastiness on your pain medication."

"Don't patronize me, dammit. I know exactly what I said and pain had nothing to do with it unless you count the one you're giving me." The hell it didn't, but Whit wasn't about to admit any weakness in front of his brother or Gracie.

He closed his eyes. If he pretended to fall asleep, maybe everyone would leave. He was pretty sure his head hurt more from his own thoughts than from the concussion. He'd done a lot of thinking after Wes and Hutch gave him hell about giving up with Gracie. He was no quitter and being called one made him mad enough to prove them wrong. Exactly what the wily bunkhouse buddies had intended, he realized later. Next thing he knew, someone was dragging him out of his wrecked truck. After that, he didn't remember anything until he woke up and saw Gracie sitting there with damp eyes and concern written all over her face.

He listened to Gracie's hushed voice now as she brought Brody up to date. "The doctor said Whit has to stay overnight for observation. Wes and Hutch will bring him back to the ranch tomorrow afternoon, if the doctor releases him. Since he won't be able to work for a while, I think he should stay in the big house. That way, Rena and I can take care of him."

Whit's eyes flew open. Take care of him? In her house? Huh-uh, not gonna happen.

"Not that I don't appreciate the offer, Gracie," he quickly interjected, "but I'll manage just fine in the bunkhouse." Might as well get the matter settled before he left the hospital. "Wes and Hutch will be around if I need anything. Besides, I don't plan on being laid up for long."

"Nonsense," she argued. "You'll need good meals and the men shouldn't be expected to wait on you. Staying in the ranch house will make it easier for everyone."

"She's right," Brody said, "but I have a better idea. I'll take you back to Texas City. That way you won't be in anyone's way."

Whit sent Brody such a venomous look, the younger Lovett quickly amended his statement. "Just until you're able to work in the office again, of course."

"I'm not working for LGS any longer, remember? So don't do me any favors, little brother. I'm not going back to Texas City."

Brody stiffened. His pale eyes narrowed. "Whatever you say, Whit. But you'll regret your decision. Wait and see."

With that, he turned on his heels and strode from the room, tossing a parting shot over his shoulder. "If you come to your senses and change your mind, I'll be at the site a few more days. Gracie knows where to find me."

This time, Whit kept his comments to himself. He was too exhausted to continue the verbal fighting, but his mind wouldn't let go of Brody's last words. *Gracie knows where to find me.* The implication made Whit want to punch something, preferably his brother's face if he'd been able.

After Brody left, Gracie moved to stand beside the bed. Hands on her hips, she looked Whit in the eye and stated her ultimatum in no uncertain terms. "If you insist on staying in the bunkhouse, then Rena and I will just have to take turns staying out there with you. It's your call."

When Whit's mouth dropped open in surprise, she silently scored one for her side and savored the heady rush of winning that round. He didn't even argue when the nurse came to administer more pain medication. Another win!

She returned to her chair and watched him doze off as the medicine did its job, her thoughts jumping ahead to tomorrow when Whit would be discharged. She didn't want him to stay in the bunkhouse with Wes and Hutch. Even though she was probably making a huge mistake, she wanted him in her house where she could take care of him.

The doctor insisted it would take at least two weeks for the bruises to heal and the soreness to disappear and advised Whit to spend that time resting. Gracie intended to make sure he followed the doctor's orders. If he went back to Texas City like Brody suggested, her questions would stay unanswered. Whit owed her an explanation and she intended to hold him accountable. When visiting hours were over, Wes and Hutch came to take her back to the ranch. She told them her plans on the way home.

The sun shone bright enough the next morning to add to Whit's headache, but the main contributors to his discomfort were his two bunkhouse buddies and their concentrated effort to get him back to the ranch after his release from the hospital.

With Wes behind the wheel of Gracie's latest purchase and Hutch riding shotgun, the trip back was as close to racing on an obstacle course as Whit ever wanted to be. The old cowboy managed to hit every pot hole in the road with the well-used truck.

"Hey, take it easy," Whit pleaded from the back seat of the extended cab. He locked his jaw to keep his teeth from rattling. Only the prospect of seeing Gracie again made the wild ride endurable. He just hoped he'd still be in one piece when they got there.

Sure enough, she was waiting on the front porch when Wes stomped on the brake and the truck lurched and shuddered to a stop. Whit held his breath and let his eyes drink in the sight of her. Jeans and a yellow knit shirt hugging her curves, cinnamon-colored hair tousled as if she'd just awakened, toes peeking out from scuffed leather sandals. And those mysterious green eyes that held him captive. He savored every detail and committed them to memory.

"Sit there till me 'n Hutch can help you." Wes' gravelly voice brought Whit's daydreaming to an end.

"I can do it myself," he insisted. "I'm not helpless."

He waited for Wes to open the truck's rear door, then eased to the ground. Before he could take a step, the two men each grabbed an arm and proceeded to lead him up the walk to the steps and into the house, despite his loud protests.

"You ain't as strong as you think you are, young man," Hutch said. "Now you just lean on us and we'll get you inside in a jiffy."

Whit's bruised ribs and pounding head made him too weak to argue, but not too weak to yell when they stumbled and the three of them nearly landed in a heap at Gracie's feet.

It had to be the pain meds causing his inability to stay awake. He couldn't even make his legs work properly. He hated not being in control of his actions. Two weeks, the doctor had told him. Two weeks of bed rest and the damned pills. For cryin' out loud, how was he going to endure two weeks of being under Gracie's scrutiny? He should've put his foot down when she insisted on bringing him here, except he couldn't even walk straight, let alone stomp his foot. He knew she was right, but that didn't make it easy to accept. Living under the same roof every day, knowing he'd be sleeping just down the hall from her every night was just too much to ask of any red-blooded man, especially one with a bruised body. He wasn't used to being dependent on anyone. Made him feel like a helpless infant. He and the twins could share nap time. Not!

By the time the men and Gracie got Whit settled in bed, he gratefully swallowed his pills and immediately fell asleep.

"You sure you're gonna be okay with him in here?" Wes inched toward the door while he talked, his attention diverted by the aroma of freshly-baked cookies coming from the kitchen.

"I'll be fine. Go ahead and sample Rena's cookies. She's got coffee ready, too. I'll be along as soon as I check on the twins."

She didn't need to tell the sweet-toothed pair twice. The men hustled down the hall, leaving her with a sleeping Whit. And a lot to think about. She was glad to have the chance for some time alone with him, even if he was sound asleep.

Since she'd already checked on Max and Susie earlier and knew they were sleeping soundly, she had plenty of time to sit and contemplate her next move. If only there was a simple answer.

"You'd think having the extra money would solve all my problems," she murmured softly.

As her gaze drifted out of the window to the new shingles on the bunkhouse roof, she thought about the list of repairs she could have done now. Sure, Whit had worked endlessly to fix the things that demanded immediate attention, like the leaking roof, but she didn't intend to rely on him any longer.

"I have enough money now to manage the ranch alone. I should be happy." But she wasn't, and that was the perplexing irritant that kept her from sending Whit on his way.

She hadn't realized she spoke her thoughts aloud until Whit moaned in his sleep. She left her chair, and her reverie, to put a hand on his forehead. When his eyes flew open, she jumped back, startled. "Oh."

"Hands are sof'." His words slurred, the medication still working to keep him quiet. "S'nice." He held out a shaky hand, his eyes silently pleading for her to take it.

She wanted to. Oh, how she wanted to. Only the emotions warring within her heart kept her from slipping her hand in his, holding it close, remembering his tenderness when he'd touched her naked body and how his hands made her crazy with need.

"I thought you were asleep," she said, pretending she didn't see the invitation in his heavy-lidded eyes. She eased her conscience by blaming his action on the drugs.

"Is there anything you want? Are you hungry?" Simple questions, innocent enough, but the minute the words were out of her mouth, she knew she was in trouble.

The corners of Whit's sensuous mouth lifted ever so slightly. His eyes darkened, disturbingly dangerous. Seriously sexy. "Want you, Gracie," he mumbled sleepily. "Hungry for you. B'lieve me, not lyin' this time. Never lie to you again."

Though his words were jumbled, Gracie had no trouble understanding them. His meaning couldn't have been clearer.

Unwillingly, her gaze locked with his. Heat rushed through her body, an electrifying charge that sizzled and cracked like a high-voltage wire out of control.

She willed herself to think of the twins and the ranch that would be their home now, thanks to the money from LGS. Those were her priorities, her future, not Whit Lovett or the way he made her feel.

"But you tried to keep me from leasing the land when you knew how badly I needed the money Brody offered. Why, Whit? Did you want the ranch for yourself? With your wealth you could own any ranch in the entire state. Why couldn't you trust me with the truth?" She didn't know why she was asking him all these questions now when he obviously wasn't lucid, but they tumbled out anyway.

Whit paled at her words and struggled to speak. "But, I promise . . ." he began.

She didn't wait for his answer, suddenly afraid to hear him say something he wouldn't remember later. "Never mind," she said and quickly left the room.

What had she been thinking? This was never going to work. She'd made another bad choice, bringing Whit here. Rena would have to take his meal to him later. Gracie planned to stay far away from the cowboy in the room next to hers. Tomorrow, she'd ask him to move back into the bunkhouse. Wes and Hutch would be there when he needed help. Let them look after him. That should keep them busy for a while.

She avoided the kitchen and the questions she knew were waiting for her. Instead, she hurried to her bedroom to check on her sleeping babies. If Rena or the men thought bringing Whit to the house to stay was unusual, she'd need time to come up with a believable answer to why she changed her mind. One that would leave no doubt to anyone how she felt about Whit. Her biggest challenge was convincing herself. She leaned back in the rocker she kept near the tiny bassinets. Maybe she'd close her eyes and nap until the babies woke up. Maybe then, the ache in her bewildered heart would cease.

Chapter Thirteen

Rena knocked on the bedroom door an hour later. Startled awake, Gracie's gaze flew to the sleeping twins, but Max and Susie were nowhere in sight.

She jumped up. "Where are the twins?"

"They're in the kitchen with Wes and Hutch. Lands sakes, honey, you fell asleep sitting in that old chair," Rena chided. "Come on and get some supper. I already changed the little ones and they're getting hungry. You can eat while I get something ready for Whit. You think he'll like my chicken and dumplings?"

"I'm sure he will. Is that what you fixed for everyone? You don't need to cook special for Whit, you know. He just has to rest until the bruised ribs heal." She didn't want Whit to think they was doing anything special for him and she darned sure didn't want him to get used to being waited on.

"It won't hurt to spoil him a little, you know." Rena wiped her hands on her apron and slipped out of the room.

Gracie stopped in front of the bathroom door. "I'll be there after I wash my hands," she said, deciding it was best not to comment on Rena's remark. She didn't want to invite a repeat of the housekeeper's earlier questioning.

Gracie entered the kitchen to the sound of babies chortling merrily and two old cowboys laughing with them like proud granddads. The cheerful ruckus was music to her ears. A fist of pure happiness squeezed her heart, holding on like a permanent fixture. Tears gathered in her eyes as she watched from the doorway. She had so much to be thankful for. All she needed was right there in her kitchen. She didn't dare wish for more.

"Got the boy settled, didja'?" Hutch stopped playing with Susie and raised an eyebrow in Gracie's direction.

"Of course, we did," Rena replied when it became apparent Gracie's attention was on her children. "And believe me, he's no boy, Hutch Hutchinson. He's man enough to make me sit up and take notice, even at my age."

Hutch and Wes both guffawed loud enough to startle a cry from Susie and her brother. Rena shook a warning finger at both men.

Sheepishly, they mumbled an apology. "Didn't mean to make you mad, Rena," Wes said. "You still figure on feeding us, don't you?"

"Well," she drawled, her eyes twinkling, "you'll have to wait until I get Whit's tray ready so Gracie can take it to him."

Gracie spun around. "Oh, no, I don't have time. You take it. Please."

Rena frowned. "Now, what's so almighty important that you can't see to the poor man's mealtime? You were the one insisted on bringing him here, remember? Didn't expect to have more work pushed in my direction." Rena turned her attention to the pot of chicken and dumplings bubbling on the stove. "This meal didn't put itself on the stove, you know."

Shame stung Gracie's cheeks. She lifted a hungry Susie from her playpen and quieted her with soft words and a hug. Max continued to fuss until Hutch retrieved a squeaky, green tractor from the toy box and tossed it to the boy.

Harried and more than a little ashamed for expecting Rena to take on more responsibility, Gracie wished for extra patience and another pair of hands, but she knew neither wish was liable to come true.

"I'm sorry, Rena. Of course, I'll take Whit's meal to him as soon as I feed the little ones." She'd do it, but she didn't have to like it.

Gracie handed the still-whimpering Susie to Wes and reached for the bottles and formula. If she'd been alone, she would have given in to the hot tears of frustration threatening to spill down her cheeks. She'd been doing that a lot lately. Ever since she took that check from Brody Lovett. Ever since she'd learned that what she'd believed was the beginning of something special with Whit turned out to be nothing but a pack of lies. Ever since . . .

She shut down the memories and vowed to keep them locked away. Nothing Whit could ever say or do could make up for the hurt he'd caused her, no matter how much she wanted him.

She'd been taking care of herself most of her life, thank you very much. And she'd do it again. Watch and see. She and her new family would be just fine.

She finished feeding the babies in record time, burped them and tucked them in bed with a kiss, then made her way back to the kitchen. She didn't dare keep Whit waiting for his dinner any longer or Rena would start with the questions again.

Wide awake and hungry after his nap, Whit heard the rattle of dishes just seconds before Gracie pushed the door open with one hip and entered the room balancing a tray of food on one hand and a cup of coffee in the other. He sniffed the air. "Mmmm, something sure smells good."

"Rena cooked chicken and dumplings. Do you think you can sit up to eat?"

"For chicken and dumplings, I'd stand up and dance," he joked, knowing full well even sitting would bring a return of knife-sharp pain to his ribs. His damnable selfishness was the cause of his aching heart.

Holding his breath, he pushed himself up slowly and butt-walked backwards until he was able to rest against the headboard. He exhaled a sigh of relief. "Damn, that hurt." He tried forcing a small laugh, as if the pain was merely an inconvenience he had to put up with, but that hurt, too.

He didn't expect Gracie to sympathize, so when she sat down on the bed beside him after setting the plate on the night stand, he was hesitant to guess what would happen next. He sure as hell knew what he wished would happen, but he had enough good sense to know wishing wasn't going to bring him what he wanted. Not in this lifetime. Not unless he found a magic lamp to rub.

The next event shocked him beyond words.

Without a word, Gracie removed the plate from the tray, scooped up a mouth-watering portion of food with a fork and—

...

Sweet heaven! What is she doing? Shock reflex made him open wide when she held the fork to his mouth. When had the art of eating become so sensual? His body heat wasn't the only thing that spiked. It was all Whit could do to keep his arousal hidden under the sheets he'd yanked into a bunch. He didn't even taste the food, just chewed and swallowed. And tried not to choke.

Gracie leaned forward with another fork full of delectable chicken and dumplings and Whit forgot all about the pain in his side. Forgot he'd lied to her. Didn't give a flying fig that she despised him. Right then, her mouth was the center of his attention. Lush, soft lips close enough to kiss. His heart stuck in his throat and all he could think about was that morning by the creek when nothing mattered but the two of them and the way they'd loved each other without limits. He had a million regrets for letting that once-in-a-lifetime chance for happiness slip away. Could he possibly repair the damage his lies had done? More than anything else, he needed to try. His long-time dream for the future he'd painted in his mind's eye was only an empty canvas without Gracie.

His gaze never left her face as he took the plate and fork from her and placed it on the bed. He reached out and took her hands in his. There was only so much temptation a man could endure.

"Dammit, Gracie, do you know what you're doing to me?"

Gracie didn't answer, didn't even struggle when Whit pulled her closer. Her expression was impossible to read, but he was positive he felt her heart beating rapidly against his chest. Felt her sweet breath feather across his face. He tumbled heart-first into the seductive depths of her sea-green eyes and knew he was lost without her.

"I'm sorry, darlin'. I should have told you the truth a long time ago," he said, hurrying his words for fear she'd leave before he could get them all out.

Then, risking a slap in the face for one more kiss from her delectable lips, Whit covered her mouth with his, taking small sips of her sweetness while waiting for the rejection that never came.

Gracie pulled away from his embrace and ran out of the room, her mind refusing to acknowledge the pandemonium Whit's kiss had caused in the vulnerable region of her heart. She never should have let him kiss her, but oh, the sweetness of his mouth on hers had almost been her undoing. This was what she'd yearned for all her life. Falling for Whit had been a dream come true, until now. No one had ever made her feel so cherished, or so naïve for being easy to deceive. Whit's confession made her realize how gullible she'd been in her eagerness for love. She would never let that happen again. She'd learned her lesson very well.

Careful not to make any noise, Gracie made her way down the hall into her grandmother's bedroom, hoping no one would think to look for her there. She needed some time alone to deal with the whirlwind of uncertainty crowding its way into her conscience. Needed to compose herself before she returned to the kitchen and three pairs of curious eyes.

Hurrying into the room, she stumbled over the stack of boxes she'd left in the room weeks ago. In the confusion of Brody's arrival and the discovery of Whit's true identity, she'd forgotten all about them. Now was a perfect time to inspect them again. Maybe, just maybe, she'd find something that would give her a glimpse of her grandparents' past and her own Texas roots. At least, it would be a welcome diversion from the past few heart-wrenching moments with Whit.

Gracie selected a dusty box of papers and carried it to the solitary cane-bottomed chair next to the old, high-poster bed. She was tempted to climb up on the quilt-covered bed, but decided would be easier to work from the chair.

With the box in her lap, she began to sort through what appeared to be unimportant invoices and sales slips from years ago. Nothing she saw gave her any clue to her grandparents' personal lives. Disappointed, she set the box aside and picked up another smaller one and discovered it was full of hard-backed journals.

Curious, Gracie picked up the first one and began to read. The pages, dusty and yellowed with age, crackled as Gracie gently turned each one, her attention riveted to her grandmother's words.

Tears blurred her vision as the story of a woman forced to choose between a loveless marriage and her love for a wayward daughter came to life through Rose Castle's meticulous penmanship. And Gracie finally began to understand her mother's past.

So absorbed in the revelation of the Castle family history that she didn't hear the door open, Gracie jerked at the sound and hurriedly set the journal aside.

Whit stood in the doorway, rumpled and barefoot.

He'd never looked so vulnerable as he did now, Gracie thought. And her heart softened at the sight of him. How could she turn him away now, when she'd just learned the truth about her own past?

How could she be sure this time she would make the right choice?

"You ran away."

His voice was too soft, too sincere to be accusatory, yet Gracie felt a need to apologize. Shaking off the uncomfortable feeling of guilt, she nodded. "Yes."

"Why, Gracie? Why won't you let me explain?" Whit hesitated slightly before he stepped into the room, as if waiting for permission to enter. "Even a condemned man is allowed a last word."

"I never condemned you, Whit. Your deception did that." She looked away, afraid she'd crumble if he made one more plea. Her determination to distance herself from anything remotely connected to him was already on shaky ground. What did he want from her? Absolution for making her fall in love with a man whose identity was a complete sham? Not very likely.

She rose and went to the window, crossed her arms over her chest in that heart-guarding habit she had. Beyond the yard, the near pasture spread out like a green blanket, thanks to a recent ground-soaking rain. Clementine and Junior lay in the shade, not far from where Hercules grazed contentedly. The serenity of the scene reinforced Gracie's determination to bring the ranch to its full potential.

Had it only been three weeks ago since she'd signed the papers that made it possible for her to settle the ranch's debts? Did Whit really think she'd turn that chance away?

She heard him walk up behind her, felt him standing close enough for his warm breath to brush across the back of her neck. Shivers of desire danced along her spine. Her knees threatened to buckle and she grabbed hold of the window sill. Crazy, she almost said aloud. Crazy for wanting this man the way her mother had wanted her lover. The way her grandmother had turned to another for the love her husband refused to give. Their misplaced loves had robbed Gracie of her childhood and wreaked havoc with her mother's life, leaving Gracie with no place to belong.

She'd never let her own misplaced love endanger the lives of her babies. She would make certain they had the security of knowing where they belonged and that they were loved, even if it meant giving up her own chance for love. She would make a family for Max and Susie built on the truth, not lies. Regretfully, that life wouldn't include Whit Lovett.

Standing behind her, he saw a sob shudder through her body. Cursing under his breath, he curbed the urge to pull her against his chest and comfort her with his embrace. His hands fisted at his side while he searched his heart for the right words to say. Words that would break the barrier of distrust Gracie had built between them.

When he could no longer resist touching her, he sucked in a nervous breath and laid his hands gently on her shoulders.

"Please listen, Gracie. If you want me to leave after I've told you the whole story, then I promise I'll go. Just give me a chance to make you understand."

He took her silence as permission to continue. With a bravado that came from pure desperation, Whit slowly turned her around to face him. The tears streaming down her face tore away his last shred of hope for reconciliation. Knowing he'd hurt her beyond forgiveness caused a pain in his heart that would stay with him forever.

He swiped at a sudden dampness in his eyes and got the shock of his life when Gracie reached up to touch his cheek with trembling fingers.

"I'll listen," she whispered, "but you have to promise you'll hear my story, too."

Whit couldn't have been more dumbfounded if lightning had struck him down right then and there. He worked his throat until he finally found the voice he'd momentarily lost.

"I promise."

"Then I suggest you start, Mr. Lovett, because what I have to say won't take long."

Whit looked around for another place to sit besides the bed, but there was only the single cane-bottomed chair in the room.

Gracie followed his gaze and quickly made her choice. "I'll take the chair. You're welcome to sit wherever you'd like." She positioned herself on the very edge of the chair, back rigid and shoulders squared.

Well, hell, what kind of option was that? Whit shrugged and carefully eased his aching body down on the floor to sit at her feet. He had to look up to see her face, but if he'd been a risk-taker, he could have laid his head in her lap. He decided not to push his luck.

"A long time ago," he began, "I was a bitter corporate captive in my family's business. I knew early on that I didn't want to follow in my father's footsteps. My family is a dysfunctional bunch of money-worshipers. Sadly, at one time, I was, too. But then I discovered a hard truth. Money can't buy love. I couldn't buy my parents' love if I were the richest man in the world. They'd damn well love my money, though."

He closed his eyes for a moment, sorted out the words he needed. "I was married once to the wealthy socialite daughter of one of my father's business associates. She was exactly the kind of wife my parents wanted for me. She was beautiful, sexy, and I believed her when she said she loved me, so I married her. The ink had barely dried on the marriage license before I was divorced. All she'd wanted was the prestige of my family name and the money that went with it. I gave it to her because I really didn't care. By then, I'd decided I liked being alone much better than the false declarations of love and tawdry affairs behind my back. Callous of me, I know, but since I'd had no role model for a good marriage, I thought they were all the same. My mother gave more time and attention to her volunteer work than to her husband. My father spent so much time at his damned company, I barely knew him. I didn't want any part of that sort of relationship."

After a long pause and another deep breath for courage, he continued. "When I was fifteen, I came home from private school to find I had a new baby brother. I rebelled by running with a wild crowd and getting into some trouble. I worked at being a pain in the butt to my parents, so every summer after school, they sent me to stay with my maternal grandparents on their ranch in Kerrville. That's where I learned what love and family was supposed to mean. And that's when I knew I didn't want any part of the Lovett financial empire. I wanted a ranch of my own someday, as far away from Texas City as possible. From then on, having that ranch was my goal and I didn't intend to share it with anyone, especially another woman."

He unfolded his long legs then and as he slowly rose from where he'd been sitting at her feet, Whit took Gracie's hands and pulled her up against his chest.

With his heart slamming against his sore ribs and a desperate need to make her understand, he told her what he'd been afraid to admit from the beginning.

"Just when I thought I had my life in order, I met an extraordinary woman named Gracie by a twist of fate. For the first time in my life, something other than the acquisition of land and money became more important to me. I fell in love so hard, I didn't know what hit me. I wanted her to love me for something other than my bank account so I lied about my identity and hoped she would eventually love me, too. I never meant to hurt anyone."

"Oh, Whit," Gracie cried right before she flung her arms around his neck and kissed him.

Before he could talk himself out of it, Whit wrapped his arms around the woman he loved and kissed her back with all the love stored up inside him.

Whatever the future held after today, he'd remember this moment for the rest of his life. Gracie in his arms and the good-bye kiss that shattered his heart.

Reluctantly, Gracie lifted her mouth from Whit's. She had to stop kissing him if she ever wanted to tell him what she'd learned about her own past.

After hearing his story, her heart had cried for the boy who never knew his parents' love and for the man who believed no woman would love him without his money. How wrong he was. And how wrong she'd been to judge him so quickly.

She'd let money influence her decision when she accepted Brody's offer, an action that reinforced Whit's belief in the power of wealth versus love and made her no better than his ex-wife. She intended to correct that mistake right now. As soon as she kissed him one more time.

When their lips met this time, Gracie was the one who gave her all. She didn't want there to be any mistake about how she felt. And to make sure Whit understood, she kept kissing him until she heard him groan in surrender.

"You've told me about the real Whit Lovett," she said, her lips mere inches from his. "Now I'll tell you about the Gracie from Minnesota."

She told him about her life in Minneapolis and how her mother's alcoholism had forced her to grow up much too fast. Resentful at having to give up what other teens were enjoying, she never wanted to be responsible for anyone again and vowed she'd never be as dependent as her mother had been. Then she told Whit about her grandmother's journals and what she'd discovered there.

"My grandmother was pregnant with my mother when she chose a loveless marriage for the security it would bring her and my grandfather never let her forget her indebtedness to him. Often, when my mother was a child, he punished her for no reason at all. In my mother's desperate search for a way to escape her unhappy home life, she made a bad choice and became pregnant at an early age by a man she believed loved her, but he left her shortly after she ran away with him. After I was born, she worked briefly as a waitress, but made another bad choice when she started to drink. By the time I was old enough to work, I became her sole support and care-giver. I never knew who my father was, never even knew I had grandparents. All I knew was how to take care of a mother who couldn't take care of herself, let alone raise a child. I promised myself never to let that happen to me."

Her tears started again and this time Gracie let them fall.

"We're not so different, you and I," she said softly. "We both missed out on parental love in our lives. But I understand now why you kept your identity a secret from me. And now I understand why I needed to be sure of who I was before I could let myself love you. Believe me, money has nothing to do with loving you."

"Love me?" Whit's eyes widened. "Did I hear you right? Did you just say you love me?"

Oh, dear God, what had she done? She hadn't meant to let those words slip out yet, but now that she had, the last remnants of any doubt she might have harbored about Whit's sincerity simply slipped away. She was ready to take a chance on love – on Whit. "I believe I did," she said. "In fact, I'm positive." Please kiss me again.

Whit lifted her off her feet and whirled her around until they were both dizzy, not even noticing the pain in his ribs. He stopped beside the bed, cradled her face between his hands and looked down at her with eyes dark with desire. "Do you know how long I've dreamed of hearing you say that, sweet Gracie?"

The ragged rasp of his voice skimmed along the sensitive surface of her skin. Her nerves danced and her heart sang.

Before she could reply, they were locked in a kiss that was everything she'd ever dreamed a kiss could be. One that knocked them off their feet in more ways than one and sent them tumbling backward onto the bed. Tangled limbs, untangled clothing, and the squeak of old bed springs. None of those obstacles slowed them down.

And when they were naked, with nothing to hide from each other's gaze, Whit rose above her, covered her mouth with his and buried himself in her welcoming heat. Gracie deepened the kiss and matched his urgency. Impatient and no longer willing to wait, she took him fully, eager to share the sensations rushing through her. Their bodies became one as they rode the waves of ecstasy until they crested together, then burst into a million sparkling stars, complete, content and undeniably loved.

Later, in the quiet sweetness of afterglow, Whit leaned over to whisper in her ear. "I don't deserve you, but please believe me when I say I'll never lie to you again."

Gracie sighed a soft *Yes* and let her heart have its way. She buried her face against the warmth of his chest and for a fragile moment she dared to believe, even though the three words she longed to hear from Whit were never said.

Chapter Fourteen

Later, when Gracie finally returned to the kitchen, Hutch gave her a disapproving frown.

"Sure took a long time just to deliver that dinner tray," he said around a mouth full of Rena's tender chicken and dumplings.

"Don't talk with your mouth full and don't be fretting about Gracie, old man," Rena scolded, passing a plate of flaky, baking-powder biscuits to Wes, then motioning for Gracie to sit. "She can take care of herself. I 'spect she went back to sit with the twins for a while. A little rest now and then is good after running her legs off every day, trying to see that everything gets done." A sly grin accompanied the twinkle in the housekeeper's eye.

"Yeah, too bad Whit turned out to be such a scalawag," Wes said, slathering butter over two warm biscuits. "He sure was a lot of help around the place. We'll miss him when there's heavy work to be done."

"Hey everyone, I'm back," Gracie said, running a nervous hand through her hair before she sat. "You don't have to talk about me like I wasn't here." Grateful for Rena's suggestion, she continued quickly. "And yes, the twins were asleep, so I took advantage while it was quiet and rested. I was a bit tired, that's all." She averted her gaze, stared at her empty plate instead.

The last thing she wanted was for her friends to know where she'd been for the last hour. She had a lot of things to sort out before she was ready to let them in on the truth.

Before they parted a few minutes ago, she and Whit had briefly agreed to take their time with this new situation. A situation that put a whole new slant on the future of the Castle ranch and the people living there.

Hutch grunted. "Didn't you have a different colored shirt on a while ago?"

Blast his eagle eyes. Gracie caught the skeptical look he shot across the table at Wes. Rena raised her eyebrows in question, too, and suddenly Gracie felt like a kid caught with a hand in the cookie jar. Okay, maybe the comparison was a little too interpretive given where her hands had actually been a half-hour ago. Heat crept up to warm her cheeks. If she'd had any sense, she would've stayed in her room until her pulse quieted and her emotions were under control. If they ever would be again where Whit Lovett was concerned.

"I, uh, spilled a little of Whit's coffee on my shirt, so I changed when I went to check on the twins." She helped herself to the chicken and dumplings, abruptly changing the subject. "This looks delicious, Rena. I can't wait to have some."

Her three inquisitive friends exchanged discreet looks. To Gracie's relief, the remainder of the meal was eaten in silence.

When the men finally made their way to the bunkhouse, Gracie rushed to help Rena put the kitchen in order so she could hurry back to Whit and their unfinished business.

"I'll just be on my way now," Rena said, hanging her apron on a hook in the pantry and retrieving her purse. "But, I'll stay if you think you'll need me to help with Whit.

"No, thanks, Rena, I'll be fine. Whit's sleeping and so are Max and Susie. I'll see you in the morning." She followed Rena to the back door. "Drive carefully."

"Well, if you're sure." Rena paused in front of the door.

Was the woman ever going to leave? As much as Gracie loved her, Rena was too perceptive for Gracie to dodge her questions much longer. "I'm positive."

With a reluctant wave, Rena made her way out to her car. As soon as Gracie heard her drive away, she breathed a sigh of relief and flew down the hall, checking first to make sure the twins were sleeping soundly. Watching the two, she was reminded again how lucky she was to have such good babies.

Not willing to waste precious time fussing with makeup, she settled for hurriedly running a brush through her curls. In order to keep the conversation focused on how they were going to deal with their current situation, she needed all her wits about her and that was darn near impossible when every time Whit touched at her, a dozen bottle rockets went off inside her stomach.

She tugged her shirt in place and entered his room.

Whit sat in a chair facing the door.

"I've been waiting for you," he said softly.

Gracie's body tingled all the way down to her toes. She couldn't have stopped her reaction if her life depended on it. And in a way it did, because if she chose to believe what Whit had told her about his past and his reason for leaving his father's company, they would have to come to an understanding about the drilling being done on her land. She intended to honor the lease she signed. She only hoped the end result would bring many years of royalty checks after Brody's speculation proved true.

"I had to wait until everyone left and make sure Max and Susie were asleep."

Whit held out his arms, his gaze roaming hungrily over her body. "I thought maybe you'd changed your mind."

"Not a chance," she said softly and started across the room.

The jarring sound of someone pounding on the front door broke the sizzling currents of anticipation in the room, halting Gracie's eager trip into Whit's embrace.

Dismayed, she acknowledged the annoying interruption. "I'll be right back."

"Tell whoever it is to come back tomorrow," he grumbled.

"I have to see who it is," she said. "I won't be long." She hoped. She couldn't imagine why anyone would be calling at the ranch now. It was after seven-thirty, not the normal time most ranchers paid social calls.

The visitor was still banging on the door when she pulled it open. Brody Lovett stood there with a hand full of papers, his face an angry red. Talk about an uninvited guest.

"Brody," Gracie said, stepping aside. "Is something wrong?"

Brody burst past her, waved the papers at her and swore loud enough to wake the boys in the bunkhouse.

"You're damn right something's wrong! Where's that no-good brother of mine? I've got a fist here waiting to connect with his cheating face." He stomped down the hall toward the bedrooms, turning the air blue with his swearing.

"Stop yelling right now or you'll have to leave. I won't allow you to come into my home and wake my children by shouting obscenities." She yanked on his arm, but he shoved her aside.

That was exactly the wrong thing for Brody to do, for just as he pushed her, Whit came limping from his room ready to take his baby brother down a notch. He'd heard Brody's irate shouting as soon as Gracie let him in the door. If something was wrong at the site, Brody would have to take it up with him some other time.

He may not be in charge here, but his bruised ribs weren't going to keep him from defending the woman he loved.

"Don't ever touch her like that again, unless you want your arm broken. Understand?" He grabbed Brody by the shirt front and pulled him up until the two brothers were nose to nose. "If you have something to say, say it, but keep your voice down."

Brody made a futile attempt to swing at Whit, but missed by a mile. Hard to hit a target when it moved quicker than lightning. And Whit was quick despite his injuries.

"Stop it, both of you," Gracie cried, and rushed to separate them. "Stop right now or take your childish fighting outside." She pounded on both men with her fists. "I mean it."

Whit hesitated, the muscles in his jaw twitching. Then, with a scowl, he abruptly released Brody's shirt with a shove.

"Let's discuss this somewhere else." He sure as hell didn't want Gracie listening to what was about to be revealed.

Brody glared at his brother. "You double-crossed me, you no good, scheming bastard! You knew there was no gas vein on that land, didn't you? What kind of underhanded deal did you pull?"

He threw the papers in Whit's face.

"What does he mean?" Gracie nailed Whit with a look that sliced through his conscience and laid it open to her painful scrutiny. "What have you done to my ranch?" Sparks snapped like green fire in her wide eyes as she looked from one man to the other.

Whit blanched. Dammit, he hadn't wanted her to find out like this. Would've preferred if she never had to know, but of course, she'd have to find out sooner or later.

A dull throb of pain gathered behind his eyes, the start of a headache that added to his misery. He frowned. His injured ribs ached, too, but not as much as his heart.

He stalled for time, but Gracie persisted.

"Ask Brody," he finally said when she demanded the truth with tear-filled eyes. "He schemed from the beginning to cheat you out of your fair share of the returns. I didn't think his initial survey was thorough enough, but it wasn't until after you signed the lease that I discovered there was nothing of value underneath those particular sections of your ranch. By then, there was nothing I could do, so I added money of my own to your account."

Anger turned Brody into a shaking, red-faced sorry excuse for a man. His voice rose uncontrollably. "I should've been smart enough not to trust you with any part of this deal. You've cost the company more than the damn land is worth."

"The result would've been the same if I'd made the deal, Brody, only I would've made the offer much higher. Your survey was at fault. If you hadn't been in such a rush to grab the lease rights, you could've checked your figures more precisely."

"My figures were correct. You must've changed them."

"That's a damn lie," Whit said, his voice dangerously soft. "The numbers are your original ones. I know better than to falsify legal documents, for crying out loud."

"I've heard enough of your arguing. I want the truth, and I want it now," Gracie announced, her hands planted firmly on her hips. "If you two can't settle matters in about two minutes, I'm calling the sheriff. Now march yourselves into the kitchen. I want to get to the bottom of this mess. Go!"

Whit and Brody were too surprised at Gracie's outburst to object.

"Better do as the little gal says," Wes said from the kitchen door. "She's a holy terror when she's mad." He and Hutch stood like bodyguards, ready to defend their Gracie in any way they could.

Whit admired the hell out of the old men right then. He was satisfied Gracie would be all right with her bunkhouse boys looking after her. He didn't regret for a minute what he'd done to add to her financial security. What good was his money if he couldn't use it to make Gracie happy? His only regret was knowing he'd never be part of her future.

With Gracie at their heels, the two brothers reluctantly made their way to the kitchen and took a seat opposite each other at the big table.

Whit experienced a *déjà vu* moment as he settled back in his chair. The old-fashioned kitchen seemed to invite the kind of conversation that often ended in unresolved matters lately. This time would be no different, he feared.

"You go first, Brody, and don't waste time making excuses." Gracie conducted the discussion like a hard-nosed judge presiding over a serious-as-sin court case. Leaning back against the kitchen counter, she folded her arms across her chest and waited. No amount of talk was going to change her mind.

Wes and Hutch stationed themselves on either side of the door.

Brody jumped at the chance to tell his side of the story first. "The deal was for access to four sections mapped out on the lease agreement. Those acres sit right in the middle of the rest of a seven thousand acre lease we already acquired. They're the only thing stopping us from hitting a goldmine, Whit, and you knew that. The survey was spot-on."

Whit propped both elbows on the table and leaned forward, his steely gaze locked on Brody's flushed face. "And you were greedy enough to offer Gracie a ridiculously low amount for the use of her land, weren't you, little brother?"

"My offer was more than enough for her to operate a ranch as small as hers. She was happy with the agreement until you butted in. Now I've paid for a dead horse, thanks to you."

Gracie pushed away from the counter. She felt sick inside at what she'd heard. She couldn't believe she'd been tricked by both Lovett brothers. Had her common sense been so side-tracked by her feelings for Whit that she'd lost all common sense?

She didn't understand all the complicated lingo of what had transpired regarding her land, but she'd find out before anyone left the kitchen.

"I want you to tell me exactly what all this means," she demanded, "and do it now. And if either of you have endangered the welfare of my children because of your selfishness, you'll wish you'd never met up with a stubborn Castle woman."

Whit didn't doubt her threat for a moment. He silently cheered at Gracie's grit and determination to protect her family. If only she loved him with the same fierce passion.

"It means there won't be any royalties because there's no producing gas vein under your land, Gracie," Whit said. "The initial check you received from LGS is the only one you'll get, except for the deposits I've arranged to have made to you on a monthly basis."

"That proves you knew it was a dry well," Brody accused.

"Not at all," Whit countered. "I set up the automatic deposits after the lease had been signed. I knew Gracie would need help until she got on her feet. With that money she can hire some help, even put some aside for Max and Susie. It's hers to use however she wants."

He approached her slowly, his dark gaze leveled on her tear-bright eyes. "It's the least I could do to make up for hurting you, Gracie. I hope someday you'll understand."

Whit left with a final good-bye. Brody stomped out after him, leaving Gracie to sort out her own tangled emotions.

Both men were guilty of deceiving her, even though their motives were poles apart. Their actions made her feel gullible and unsophisticated. After all, she knew nothing about geological surveys or the affluent world that people like the Lovetts took for granted.

Still, Whit's generosity would make it possible for her to have financial security for the rest of her life. Or did he view her situation as a charity case, one he could "fix" with his wealth and ease his conscience at the same time? He certainly had no obligation to put such a ridiculous amount of money into an account simply to assure a secure future for her and the twins. Nothing about that made any sense. She couldn't let him go without finding out the real reason why he refused to stay. If he truly cared, she couldn't fault him for that. Did she even want to? Still, all the money in the world couldn't buy forgiveness — or love.

Whit stretched out on his bunk for the last time. His thoughts were as dark as the late night sky that hung over the bunkhouse. He'd already packed his duffle and the last of his personal items were ready to be tossed in his new truck at morning's first light. There was nothing left to do now but wait. For what, he wasn't quite sure. He only knew that once he left, he would never come back. His plan was to leave at daybreak before Gracie woke up. Leave before Rena rattled up the drive in her old car and hopefully, before his two geriatric sidekicks rolled out of their sacks.

God, he was going to miss them. Miss the crazy troupe that made up the Castle ranch and the family he'd come to secretly think of as his own. He'd never forget that first moment he'd helped Max and Susie into the world and how blown away he'd been by the miracle of birth. Gracie's amazing strength as a mother during those moments had opened his eyes to what true love looked like.

Sadness settled over him like a dark blanket, shutting out all hope for a brighter tomorrow. No tomorrow would ever be bright without Gracie and her little ones to share it.

When he finally realized Brody brought an offer to the table less than the company policy allowed simply because Gracie was a woman, Whit advised her not to sign. But Gracie had jumped at the chance for the money without checking into what other ranchers were being paid. If only she'd asked Whit's advice, he would've helped her. But she didn't trust him enough for that.

As soon as she found out he'd lied about his identity, she'd labeled him untrustworthy. He admitted she'd been right. So he'd done the best he could to rectify his bad judgment by adding a huge amount to the original bank deposit from LGS, as well as arranging for regular monthly deposits to be added to her bank account from his own. Brody agreed to pull his equipment out and sign the lease back to Gracie since a dry hole was useless to the company. She was never supposed to find out the money came from him. So much for well-laid plans.

In the past few weeks, he'd watched Max and Susie thrive on Gracie's love and devotion and learned that being their surrogate mother didn't matter to her. She loved them unconditionally. She was a terrific parent, in spite of all the tough circumstances she'd struggled to overcome. He'd never loved anyone the way he'd come to love Gracie. Never lost his heart so easily or so completely. All he'd ever wanted to do was give Gracie the things she'd missed in her life. He knew now, those material things he'd always taken for granted were not as important to her as honesty, faith in each other and above all, unconditional love. She counted her riches in ways that would last a lifetime. He was the one who'd missed out on the best things in life.

Swearing softly to keep from waking the bunkhouse boys down the hall, Whit shoved off the cot and reached for his boots. Might as well hit the road now. No reason to put it off.

From where Gracie sat on the back porch, she could make out the shadow of the outbuildings. There was enough moonlight to illuminate the window of the room she knew belonged to Whit.

Movement inside captured her attention. She left the chair to stand at the edge of the porch and lean forward to see better.

Someone was moving around. She took a closer look and gasped. The familiar figure was clearly visible and after a trip to his truck and back, Gracie guessed what he had in mind. He was leaving! She hadn't really believed him when he'd said good-bye. Hadn't thought about how miserable life would be without him.

After she'd heard his reason for undermining Brody's deal, she was able to understand better. Whit cared, something she'd known all along but wouldn't let her wary heart believe. And her distrust was driving him away. Remembering all the special times they'd shared in the short time they'd been together.

She flew down the path, slowing her steps as she approached the closed door to his room. With a trembling hand, she quietly turned the knob and slipped inside.

Whit stood in the shadowed room, unmoving, as she walked toward him. He held his duffle in one hand, his hat in the other.

"Please don't leave," she whispered. "I need you, Whit. We all do."

Uncertain what his reaction would be, Gracie waited on unsteady legs, her hands clasped in front of her, her heart pounding so loud she was certain he could hear it.

"Gracie," Whit murmured, his voice breaking. His eyes held an undisguised plea for forgiveness that shook her to the core, tearing away the last remnants of doubts.

She moved closer, the duffle bag he held slid to the floor and his hat landed on the narrow table by the door.

Unable to deny herself the need to touch him any longer, she raised her arms to circle his neck. Standing on tiptoes, she tenderly touched her lips to his.

The earth moved as rockets exploded in the darkness of the tiny room. Whit rolled his mouth over hers, his tongue begging for entry. Willingly, she complied, her own tongue danced with his to the same earthy, suggestive tempo that rocked their straining bodies.

"I couldn't let you leave. Not yet. Not until you convince me you truly don't want to stay."

He took so long to answer, Gracie was positive her knees would've collapsed beneath her trembling body if he hadn't been holding her. The goddess of good fortune must have been smiling on her, though, because Whit drew her close and kissed her in that all-consuming way he had of setting her body on fire. This time the flames burned higher than ever, hot enough to burn the past and bright enough to light the future. She'd made the right choice and prayed Whit would, too.

"I'll stay forever if you let me, sweet Gracie," Whit said, picking her up and carrying her to his bed.

Gracie smiled up at him. "Forever isn't long enough," she said, easing one hand under his belt buckle, "but if you've got the time, so do I."

The belt slid away, along with the rest of their clothes. "How much time do you have right now?" he asked, his hands busy caressing her supersensitive breasts.

She shuddered as he thumbed them, kissed their rosy peaks, then slid his kisses down her abdomen to other, more sensitive parts. "I've got all the time in the world," she gasped in wonder while he shared secret pleasures with her.

Whit loved her tenderly, giving her what she needed—what she didn't even know she wanted until a volcano erupted from the very center of her being, and she realized she'd never have this kind of love again. She was ready for him and eager to please him in every way. And to his intense gratification, that's exactly what she did.

Whit was sure he'd died and gone to heaven. His body ached in places that had no connection to his accident. In fact, he was certain his bruised ribs had healed because he didn't feel a one of them. He was happier than he'd ever been in his thirty-two years. Thank God, Gracie had a forgiving heart and the amazing ability to love him, even with all his shortcomings.

A faint light gilded the bed in a golden glow. Was it the sun? Surely not. Whit bolted upright, stared the morning sun in its face and swore.

"Gracie," he touched her shoulder. "Sweetheart, it's morning. What about Max and Susie?"

Gracie shot out of bed and grabbed her clothes, dancing on one foot, then the other, as she dressed. "Oh, no! What kind of mother am I?" She raked a hand through her tousled locks. "What if they're awake? They won't know where I am. What if they're scared and crying?"

She ran out of the bunkhouse with one shoe on, holding the other and chastising herself all the way to the back door.

She burst into the kitchen and was met by the aroma of steaming coffee and sizzling bacon filling the room. Wes and Hutch were busy at the stove, cooking breakfast like they knew what they were doing. Max and Susie chortled happily in their playpen with a mountain of toys that looked suspiciously new.

Shocked and more than a little mortified, Gracie stared at the scene of domesticity her dear bunkhouse boys created and couldn't help the tears that flowed. Tears she'd held back for way too long. Tears of love for these men and their bumbling, caring ways.

"Hey, young lady, no need to carry on so," Hutch said, a hitch in his gravelly voice sounding more like a lion with a sore throat. "Ever'thing's under control. Me 'n Wes fed the little ones and even put on their dry diapers. Rena'll be here directly, so we figured we'd let her get them dressed." He puffed out his chest. "I think we done a good job."

Gracie flew to Hutch and gave him a big hug. "You've done a wonderful job, but I don't understand. How'd you know?" She blushed.

Wes winked knowingly. "Heard you and Whit talking last night and we figured we'd best get up here to the house and watch over the young'uns while you two settled your differences. 'Bout time, too." He put the platter of bacon and eggs on the table. "Bet you're hungry, huh?" His teasing grin sent more heat to Gracie's already blushing face.

Hutch poured coffee and set the mugs out just as Whit came rushing through the door.

"Well now, that look on your face is priceless, Lovett," Hutch said. "What were you expecting to see?"

Whit's deep laugh joined Gracie's softer one as he planted himself right next to Gracie. "Not this scene, for sure, you sly old foxes." He looked down at Gracie. "Guess we didn't fool anyone, did we?"

Gracie shook her head. "Only ourselves, Whit. Only ourselves." She picked up Susie, kissed her chubby cheek and handed her to Whit, then took Max in her arms and blew a kiss on his bare belly. Max giggled, then screwed up his face and filled his diapers.

"Thanks for not giving me that one," Whit grinned and rocked Susie in his arms. "Little girls are definitely more polite than little boys."

Gracie made a face at Whit and disappeared to take care of Max.

Whit sat down at the table and motioned for Wes and Hutch to join him. Susie was happy to snuggle in the cradle of his arms.

"I suppose you two want to know what's going on between Gracie and me, huh?"

Wes set his cup down, stroked his bristly chin. "Well, can't say as we're surprised. But we've sure been wondering if you two would ever come to your senses. Now the next question is what took you so long and what do you intend to do about it?"

Whit cleared his throat. "I guess the next step is asking her to marry me, if she'll have me."

"That's right," Wes said. "Reckon you better get busy on that right away."

Hutch enthusiastically nodded his agreement. He helped himself to bacon, cocking his head as the rattle of tires on gravel told them their favorite cook was back.

All three looked toward the door as Rena marched in, arms loaded with grocery bags, as usual.

"What in heaven's name have you done to my kitchen?" She eyed the counter littered with enough dirty pans to cook a banquet. Finding an empty spot, she set the bags down. With her hands on her hips, she skewered the men with a look that made them both hang their heads. "Who's the culprit and why couldn't you have waited for me to get here?"

They all talked at once until Rena finally held up her hands. "One at a time, for goodness sake. Whit," she glared at him, "you can start by telling me why you, of all people, are holding Susie. You've never held either one of the babies in all the time you've worked here."

It took nearly five minutes and numerous interruptions from Wes and Hutch before Whit got the entire story told about what had transpired the previous night.

Rena plopped down in the nearest chair and fanned her face.

"Well, all I can say is when's the wedding?"

The Castle Ranch — Nine months later

Springtime in the Texas Hill Country is a beautiful season when bluebonnets nod their heads while mockingbirds sing and chase the squirrels from the safety of their trees.

This morning, Hercules bellowed his happiness at having three new cows added to his harem. He would only be slightly disappointed at his part in increasing the ranch's herd. New calves scampered and played near their mamas. The Castle ranch was thriving. Thanks to implementing the use of AI, Whit had been able to offer the prize bull's services in an entirely new and profitable way. There'd be no gas lines on the Castle Ranch's land, only pasture for the outstanding herd of cattle he and Gracie were developing.

Whit's father, the owner and president of Lovett LGS, had handed the company over to his youngest son, who gladly accepted the position. He renamed the company BRODY SUNSHINE ENTERPRISES, changing its direction as an experimental endeavor, developing retirement communities along the Gulf Coast.

Elated not to be a part of the company any longer, Whit wished his brother good luck. He had an endeavor of his own in the works that beat anything Brody Lovett could ever imagine. Damn straight!

After showing four new hired hands around the ranch and getting them settled, Whit hurriedly finished some paper work in the newly constructed building where AI procedures were done before he headed for the house for a brief break. On his way, he did a lighthearted shuffle when he thought about the future.

Gracie sat on the front porch of the newly painted house waiting for Whit to come in from the barn.

Nine-month old Max and Susie babbled and squealed from their play pen as soon as they saw the man who would most certainly, swoop down, lift them up and swing them around. He always did.

In the kitchen Rena rattled pots and pans, keeping up a steady stream of gossip with Wes and Hutch, both men happy to be relieved of their outdoor chores. Sitting in the kitchen with a cup of Rena's coffee and a piece of her cinnamon coffeecake was the highlight of their day. They'd make it last all morning, if they could.

Whit made his way up the path, stomped his boots on the wire dirt catcher, then made quick work of crossing the porch to take his wife in his arms and kiss the daylights out of her. Every day, he gave thanks for the wonderful life he'd been blessed with.

True, his money made part of it possible, but it was Gracie's love that made it all worthwhile. He kissed her again, in no hurry to end the moment. "Mrs. Lovett, have I told you lately that I love you?"

He was answered by the lusty shouts from a pair of very insistent children, so he gathered them up in his arms like they knew he would. He was quickly smothered in kiddie kisses.

Gracie favored her husband with a smile bright enough to light up the entire state of Texas. "Not nearly enough, Mr. Lovett." She lifted her face for another kiss and relieved him of tiny Susie, who protested for only a minute before snuggling against her mama's shoulder.

Whit's passion for Gracie burned as fiercely as the first time they'd kissed. He tenderly stroked her barely rounded belly and his heart overflowed with love for this woman who had changed his empty life and made it a safe haven for his heart.

"I think it's time to make the announcement, don't you?" Pride and love rushed through Whit like an emotional tidal wave.

"I'm sure it won't come as a surprise," Gracie said, laughing softly. "Rena's been commenting on my morning sickness and her sharp eye doesn't miss a thing, but let's do it anyway."

Whit grinned proudly. "I've been thinking, darlin'. Why don't we ask the bunkhouse boys to be our new baby's godparents. Rena, too, if she's willing." With Max in one arm, Whit circled Gracie and Susie with his free arm, holding all three close, cherishing them just like he'd promised in his wedding vows. Like he intended to keep on doing as long as he had breath in his body.

Gracie laid her head in the curve of his shoulder and sighed. "That's a wonderful idea, Whit. Let's go ask them now."

She started to go, but Whit held her for a moment longer. Whispered in her ear, "The sooner we get the meal over with, the sooner I can take you to bed and show you how much I love you."

Gracie hugged him and laughed. "Sorry, but it's not even lunch time yet. You'll have to take a number this evening," she teased. "Then you can be next in line right after the twins have had their baths and are put to bed. I promise."

Desire darkened Whit's eyes, love for his wife made them shine. "You mean *I'll* be next in line for a bath and bed, don't you? That's hours away," he moaned, pulling a forlorn look.

Gracie laughed and impatiently pushed Whit through the door. "That's not what I meant, Whit Lovett. Now let's get this day moving or there won't be enough time left for us."

"I could live to be one hundred and there'd still never be enough time for loving you, sweet Gracie."

"Well, let's not waste time," she said. "I see a very special bath time in your future."

Max and Susie giggled in their forever family's arms.

Today was turning into a very good day at the Castle.

*****THE END*****

About the Author

Loralee Lillibridge, is a long-time fan of romance novels and a strong believer in the power of love. She grew up in Texas loving cowboys and rodeos, but relocated in Michigan after her marriage to a handsome Yankee who stole her heart.

She still favors country love songs, and seeing a field of Texas bluebonnets can make her cry, but she admits the West Michigan lakeshore has a beauty all its own.

Even as a child, Loralee's love of books, combined with a vivid imagination, fueled a desire to create her own stories with characters readers could care about. Her first attempt was a neighborhood play about a pirate who rescued a princess. (Original, yes?) Needless to say, the audience only consisted of her parents and the boy next door who reluctantly played the role of the pirate.

Now she enjoys writing emotionally fulfilling stories centered on the relationship of a man and a woman and their often rocky road to love. Heart-warming stories of ordinary people and extra-ordinary love.

Visit Loralee at:

www.loraleelillibridge.com

Tell-Tale Publishing would like to thank you for your purchase. To read more by Loralee or other fine TT authors, please visit:

www.tell-talepublishing.com

www.ingramcontent.com/pod-product-compliance
Lightning Source LLC
Chambersburg PA
CBHW071259190726
48292CB00007B/2613